AUCTIONED TO THE LUMBERJACKS

A LUMBERJACK REVERSE HAREM ROMANCE

STEPHANIE BROTHER

ISBN: 9798873352609

CHAPTER 1

SKYE

SELLING MY SOUL

"You're next." The man beside me looms in the darkness, his face shadowed and emotionless.

My heart beats so fast against my ribcage that it makes me breathless. I scan the room as the overwhelming scent of smoke, alcohol, and stale man increases my panic. There's another woman on the platform, illuminated by a bright light. Somewhere out of sight, a man is taking bids, his voice rumbling with each price increase. She's not like me, though. She's forced into this, but I've chosen to be here. The price she achieves will go to an unseen owner. My bidder will promise the money directly to me.

I focus on calming my racing pulse, breathing in for five and out for ten. In. Out. My palms hurt, and I glance down, finding my nails have marked grooves into my skin. I can't think straight. My mind is a racing whir of thoughts, tangled with emotions, threatening to overwhelm me unless I get a grip.

I'll be out there in a minute, displayed to a room full of men, set to be auctioned to whoever is willing to pay the highest price. Good man or bad, handsome, or ugly, I won't have a choice. The arrangement is for a year of my life.

I strain to make out some of the faces of the men in the crowd, shuddering at the leering expressions. The girl on the platform is dressed in a tight black dress, which leaves next to nothing to the imagination. I glance down at my jeans and simple black tank, wondering if my clothes will work for me or against me.

My lips feel sticky with the lipstick I applied with trembling fingers. Beneath my arms and down my back, I'm already slick with sweat. I sway, gripping the arm of the man who will shortly send me to my fate. He shakes me off with a look of utter detachment, and tears burn in my throat.

I'm alone.

Alone and empty in a way I can't even quantify. Where my heart used to be is just a bottomless pit of sorrow that can't be filled.

I'm brittle and untouchable. Numb and hollow.

The only thing keeping me together is knowing that whatever happens next won't hurt as much as what I've already been through. This decision, although risky and crazy, is my only path to becoming whole again.

"You're up!" He nudges me forward and stays close behind as I force one foot in front of the other until I'm on the platform. The light is so bright that I have to squint, and even then, I can't see anything in front of me.

The bidding begins, and with every rumble of the auctioneer's voice, I feel closer to passing out.

I remember what the auction organizer advised: just be yourself in the moment to attract the most suitable bidder. A natural match, he said, as though I had a chance of finding my knight in shining armor, my Mr. Right.

Being shy or nervous isn't necessarily a deterrent, he told me. Far from it. Men like this, the ones out there wanting to exchange money for flesh, like their women to be docile and subservient. The thought brings bile to my throat.

Struck with the sudden realization that this is my only chance to raise the funds I need, I'm gripped by a need to give it my best shot.

"Do you want some of this?" The once detached steward offers me his small silver flask, which I take gratefully. I don't know what is in it, but it burns the back of my throat and settles into my stomach with unsettling warmth.

Male voices rumble, and the acoustics bounce the sound through my head to my feet and ground me to the spot. I can't be scared. I can't be ashamed or embarrassed. I have to be determined.

I turn with panic surging through me, giving everyone a three-hundred-and-sixty degree view of what they can buy. If there is one thing I'm sure of, it's that I'm attractive. Not in a film star way, but my girl-next-door innocence has always appealed to the kind of men who have wanted to corrupt me.

My chestnut waves settle around my shoulders, and I position my face as if in defiance. I keep my eyes focused in front of me, even though the crowd is dark.

Then, as though a surge of electricity momentarily interrupts the spotlight glaring into my eyes, the crowd becomes visible for a second. Directly in front of me are three huge men with stern faces half covered by unruly beards. Two have their beefy arms folded across their chests. The other, his thumbs hooked into the pockets of his jeans. I blink, then squint as the light glares again, and they disappear, but this time, I know who's looking at me, and somehow, that pushes a lightning strike of nerves right through me. I sway, reaching out to grab something to stabilize myself but finding nothing. My heartbeat swells like the beat of a bass drum, my lungs constricting so tightly, I gasp. As my vision closes in, I hear the word sold, and everything goes dark.

When I blink again, my vision is dark around the edges, and my mouth is dry and sour. I squint through the tunnel of darkness, becoming aware of a hazy figure standing over me. I hear my voice like a distant echo. "Where...where am I?"

"Here, sip this. You blacked out." A huge man, Herculean almost, rests a glass of water against my lips. His hand lifts my head until I'm propped up enough to drink. The water is ice cold, sending a shiver through me that rattles my bones. There's a kindness behind his soft gray eyes, which catches me off guard. It's been a long time since anyone looked at me with anything other than disdain.

I scan his face, his tumble of fair hair, the bushiness of his beard, and the sinew and strength of his upper arms that stretch the fabric of his shirt to almost breaking point. His big legs strain against worn jeans as he squats to take care of me. Glancing down, I notice I'm covered with a jacket that I assume is his.

"Is she coming with us or what?" The voice sounds from behind me, and I swivel, staring up into a harder, meaner, older face. Where his friend's eyes are filled with kindness, this man looks at me as though I'm a stray dog he intends to kick into a ditch.

"She's coming. Give her a chance."

I scramble against the sticky fabric of the liver-colored leather couch, gathering my wits. I want to ask who these men are, but my lips are frozen closed. Another man across the room rises from a small wooden chair. His close-cropped hair, dark beard, and intense dark eyes make me instantly fearful. "We need to get out of here. This place..." He shakes his head as though he's as disgusted with the auction process as I am. "You're coming with us."

"Where?"

"It's three hours from here. A cabin on a beautiful mountain surrounded by the most stunning forest you've ever seen." The man who's still holding the water smiles at the memory, but the remoteness of his description doesn't hold the same appeal to me.

I thought I'd be staying in the city. I thought I'd be close to Hallie, even if I have no way of seeing her.

The second man taps his foot, restless and coiled tight with resentment.

"But there are three of you," I snap. "Who bid for me?"

"We all did." The man with cropped hair reaches out to take my arm and help me up. "I'm West. That's Finn." He nods at the friendly man who rises to his feet at the same time as me. "And that's Jack."

Jack scowls at the mention of his name as though he'd rather I didn't know anything about him.

"I didn't agree…" I trail off, realizing that it's pointless to dispute the terms and conditions of my agreement to participate in this exchange of money for me. The auctioneer has accepted their payment, and I'm not in any position to object. I keep my chin high, wanting them to know I'm not weak and broken, even though that's precisely what I am. If they think they can destroy me, they will.

"We paid extra," Finn says. "Three of us. Three times the work."

He says work with emphasis that makes me imagine something grueling and harsh. The contract states I will cook, clean, and provide physical services to meet their needs. Doing that for one man was an overwhelming prospect, but three?

"Extra?"

"Three times the final bid."

I sway on my feet as the prospect of triple the money I was hoping to achieve registers. I'll have enough to do what is necessary. This—whatever I'm going to have to do for the money—will be worth it.

Jack looks at me briefly, but his eyes don't settle and his gaze flits between his companions and the door.

The auctioneer interrupts the intensity of the moment with a knock on the door. He holds in his red, meaty hands two envelopes of paper. One is given to Jack and one to me. "As agreed, the money is held in an account in your name, but you won't be able to access it for a full year. All the details are in here."

Jack looks at the envelope with eyes so angry, I'm surprised it doesn't turn to dust in his hands.

"Thanks. We're ready to go." West turns his attention to me. "Where are your things?"

"I only have a purse."

Jack mumbles an expletive under his breath and walks out the door, not waiting for anyone else. Finn touches my arm. "Go get your purse."

As I leave the room, he follows me. I guess he's worried I'm going to run. He doesn't realize that I have nowhere to run to.

In the room where the women gather before the auction, I find my purse. In the corner, a girl who doesn't look any older than me quietly sobs. I want to reach out to her and let her know that as long as she's living and breathing, everything has a chance to get better. It's what I tell myself in all the moments I've felt like I've hit rock bottom and broken through to even greater misery. It's the only thing that's kept me going. But I don't say a word because my problems are waiting for me outside, and I don't have anything left in me to give to a stranger.

Finn walks beside me as we make our way from the building and into the night. I shiver, and he rests his coat around my shoulders like a man on a date, not someone taking his glorified sex-slave back to his remote cabin in the woods. Fear and trepidation consume me, and my knees feel like they could go out from beneath me. My breathing is labored, and Finn's hand, which suddenly grips my elbow, is the only thing that keeps me from falling.

West unlocks a truck that reminds me too much of Carter's, causing slick dread to slide down my spine, but I don't have time to think before Finn opens the rear door and firmly helps me inside.

The interior is illuminated by a small light that casts the back of Jack and West in an eerie yellow glow. Their oversized frames fill the front seat, their plaid-covered shoulders almost touching across the space between their seats. Finn rounds the vehicle and slides in next to me, his eyes trailing my face and body as I fasten my seatbelt and pull the coat closer around me. The truck rumbles to life, and through the window, I watch as the places I'm familiar with pass in a blur.

"We're going to go to a store to buy you what you need." West's voice breaks through the silence, making me jump.

My instinct is to tell him that they don't have to spend their money on me, but I can't live in this one outfit for a year. I could apologize for leaving all my worldly possessions behind, but then I'd have to explain what I'm running from, and that isn't something I'm prepared to confide.

I rest my head against the car and close my eyes, too overwhelmed to face the future that's rushing towards me like a swinging ax. I focus on my breathing and the whooshing of blood in my ears until everything around me fades to black.

The next time I come to my senses, I'm lying down against the rough fabric of the seat. Voices skitter on the edge of my consciousness. "She's literally got nothing, man," Finn says.

"She doesn't need much," Jack says. "It's not like she's going anywhere."

I swallow against the tight constriction of my throat.

"I have some shirts she can have," Finn says.

7

"They'll swamp her." West makes a gravelly sound in his throat. "Have you seen how small she is?"

"Small enough to break."

Finn stiffens next to me at Jack's comment. "She's brave, Jack. So damned brave to do what she did. The rest of those girls didn't have a choice but she…she chose to be there."

"Brave?" It's a word accompanied by a scoff. "Stupid, more like."

"Yeah, well. We don't know her story."

"And we don't need to know. This whole thing…I told you it wouldn't end well. It hasn't even begun well. But you need to make sure you keep boundaries in place. She's not your girlfriend. She's not a friend. She's an employee at best, and she's going to work for her money. Don't go thinking you can treat her kindly because that's fucked up…giving the poor girl false hope and expectations you're never going to fulfill."

West must signal because the truck makes a ticking sound and then slows to a stop.

"Is she awake?" he asks Finn.

"She's sleeping."

West mutters something and then throws the door open, closing it as quietly as he can. Finn exits the vehicle as well, leaving me trapped in a truck with a man as angry as Carter was when I told him I was leaving. The look in his eyes was as dark as the depths of the underworld.

I lay totally still, keeping my breathing even, praying Jack doesn't realize I'm awake. Minutes that feel like hours stretch tight around me. My legs ache from being cramped, and my face itches, but I fight the urge to do anything about either.

After what I think must be fifteen minutes, a rumble of motorbike engines surrounds us, vibrating the truck and the air around me. Pretending to sleep amid such overwhelming noise would be stupid and potentially make Jack doubt my honesty in the future. I open my eyes and uncurl so I can see what's happening. Jack lowers his window.

The motorcycle engines cut, and five leather-clad men remain seated on their vehicles as they remove their helmets and rest them on the handlebars of their bikes.

Their ragged beards and hair are more unruly than the lumberjacks, and a couple of them sport large bellies which hang over their belted leather pants. The others look as toned and muscular as the lumberjacks, covered with ink and wearing leather cuts that read Shadow Outlaws around a sinister-looking insignia.

Finn approaches confidently and embraces one of the biker men warmly. They clearly know each other and there is no threat that I can sense. "Hey, cuz," he says, clapping the man on the shoulder. The resemblance between them becomes clear.

Their conversation fades as a huge biker, who's taller and more powerfully built than even Finn, approaches the window.

"Hey, Jack. We missed you last week at Reggie's!"

"Yeah, sorry about that, Bones. Work is taking over. What are you lot here for?"

"You know, a few bottles and some tobacco. Nathan's missus is out of town so we're playing poker. Join us if you like."

"We've got some stuff going on tonight."

Jack jerks his head and Bones narrows his eyes, focused on where I'm huddling in the back seat, shadowed but still visible in the low light from the shop sign. His eyebrows shoot up.

"Pretty little thing," he says.

Jack shrugs like my attractiveness is neither here nor there.

"We'll catch up soon."

"No problem, man!" Bones grapples in one of his pockets and pulls out bundle of bills, handing some over to another one of the group who ambles into the store, stopping to talk to West as he emerges from the entrance.

I lower myself back down, trying to be as silent as I can and moments later, Finn and West are back in the truck, bringing a blast of icy night air with them.

I shudder and curl into a ball again, fearing and dreading a cold hand on my neck.

West stuffs the rustling bags at Jack's feet.

I must've fallen asleep again because I'm disturbed as a rough hand, like sandpaper delivering the lightest touch, grazes my forehead. I blink in the darkness, forgetting where I am for a moment, and then jump when I wake fully. Finn is braced with his hands up, palms facing me. "We're home."

I look around, finding only inky blackness around us. I can barely see anything outside the glass.

Finn smiles, but it feels more like nerves than happiness.

I've done what I need to do. The money is within my grasp. All I have to do is get through the next three-hundred-and-sixty-five days, and then I'll be free.

Home.

As West and Jack disappear into the darkness, and Finn urges me out of the car, I wonder if I'll ever find a place I can truly call home again.

CHAPTER 2

WEST

BOUGHT AND PAID FOR

My legs have seized on the journey, but the distance from the truck to the front door of the lodge loosens them. I clutch the bag of items I bought for the woman who's trailing behind with Finn, feeling uncertain about what I picked out for her. It was the first time I ever had to choose underwear and sleepwear for a woman. The clothing selection wasn't huge, but I got a few vests, sweaters, leggings, jeans, and woolly socks. Finn told me her shoe size, and I found a pair of warm boots that should fit. Maybe she'll like everything. Maybe she won't. She'll have to wear it all, regardless.

I throw open the rustic wooden door, and the smell of home hits me in the face: pine, burning wood, and dust. We've done our best to keep it habitable, but none of us are winning any housekeeping awards. The sound of three sets of feet crunching over leaves and stumbling over roots

11

disturbs the silence of the forest, but no one talks. The atmosphere is thick with anticipation, and everything that remains unsaid between me and my two friends, and the stranger who has come to join us in our home.

This is no small thing that we've done, and it wasn't an overnight decision. We all acknowledged that we could do with a woman around the place to make this house a home, but how to achieve it was a hot topic of discussion. Finn misses the affection of a woman the most. Jack was opposed from the start. Women are trouble in his eyes. They can't be trusted. He didn't want to bring complications into our simple life, but it was two against one, and he's fed up with dealing with all his pent-up frustrations himself.

Now, I feel as though I have something to prove to dismiss his reservations. The auction was the only way I saw we could achieve our goal. It's not like three men can wander into a bar and proposition one woman. The sight of us with our big beards and giant hands would likely scare off even the most eager of women. Putting our attractiveness aside, there's no refinement in this house. No romance, that's for sure.

And what we need from this woman isn't hearts and flowers. Paying for it makes everything clear-cut. She's signed on the dotted line. She'll have to get used to giving us what we need, and if she resists, we'll bend her to our will or send her back with nothing.

Jack lumbers behind me, and his vibes are as menacing as ever.

Finn ushers the woman inside, and she glances around like a frightened rabbit, watching close the door behind her with wide eyes and parted lips. Then, as if conscious of being watched and appearing scared, she straightens her shoulders and lifts her chin.

Her rigid spine and a hint of defiance make my cock thicken.

"What's your name?" It's a question I should have

asked back at the auction, but I wasn't thinking straight. She's so pretty; just looking at her glitches my mind into dark places that, if she knew, would probably set goosebumps across her skin.

"Skye." Her sweet, feminine voice sounds strangely beautiful within the confines of our rustic home. I'm used to Jack's growl and Finn's deeply smooth tones.

"Pretty," Finn says. Jack scowls in response.

I watch Skye slowly scan the interior, taking in the hand-built kitchen and large table that still looks very much like the tree it was sliced from, the worn couch, and the wide beams that span the ceiling overhead. In the corner, a woodburning stove glows with lingering cinders. She seems to be holding her breath but making a good show of confidence. I see the cabin from her eyes and feel renewed pride in the cozy home we've managed to build from the ground up. Admittedly, it's sparse and without the benefit of a woman's touch, something I'm hoping Skye will rectify over her time here.

She's yours for a year. You can do anything to her, and she has to submit if she wants the money. The whisper in my mind sends a thrill down my spine, making my balls tighten.

I wonder how she'll feel about dropping to her knees and taking my cock deep into her throat. Will she cry out when I slap her ass until it's as red as the sunset? Will she cry when Jack ties her up and does unspeakable things to her in the hope that she'll beg him for mercy?

If there's one thing I learned from being in the military, it is that setting boundaries and expectations has to be done immediately. There's no settling-in period. No chance to go easy on Skye if we expect her to know her place in this cabin going forward.

"You know why you're here," I say, stepping closer to her. Skye's green eyes flash with uncertainty, but she grits her teeth before speaking.

"I know."

Finn clears his throat, but I shoot him a warning look

13

over Skye's head. I know him. He wants to backtrack. He doesn't understand the risk. We take her and break her in tonight, or we risk this whole thing falling apart.

"Take your things. Get ready. You have ten minutes." I hold out the bag, and she reaches out for it, her hand shaking just a little before she steels herself. "Your room is the second door on the right. The bathroom is across the hall."

Part of me expects her to object or at least ask for time to settle in first. She's barely exchanged two words with us. But it turns out Skye has more backbone than I thought. Either that, or this situation she finds herself in isn't new.

The thought of her being touched by the hands of another man fills me with instant rage. It's fucked up that I already think of her as mine, but I do.

When she leaves the den, and I hear a door click shut, I turn to Finn. "Just remember what we spoke about."

"I warned him," Jack says. "Now it's real, he's already going soft."

"I'm not." Finn juts out his jaw and focuses on me. "I know what you said, but Skye isn't some brassy, experienced woman. She's soft and fragile."

"There's nothing fragile about that girl. Did you not see her grit her teeth? She was biting back a mouthful of resistance that we need to squash before it escapes." Jack slumps into the brown cord couch, spreading his legs and stretching his arms above his head.

"You're young," I remind Finn. "You haven't seen what we've seen."

"I've seen plenty." His eyes drift to the doorway Skye disappeared through, the craving in them so palpable that I have to look away. Finn's an orphan, and he lost his momma too young. It's made him weak for the affection of women, but this experience is going to banish that.

Thirst urges me to the sink, where I pour myself a tall glass of water, downing it in gulps. I stare out of the window into the black expanse of the forest, craving the cool air and atmosphere of calmness between the trees. These men have become like brothers, but living with them isn't always easy. Living without them would be harder, so we make it work. Family can be like that.

Turning back, I find Finn hovering like he doesn't know whether to sit or stand. He's jittery, gnawing at the edge of his thumb and flexing his other fist at his side.

"Let me take the lead," I say, not trusting either of the other men to know how to handle this situation. Finn will go in too soft and Jack too hard. Skye's going to need a firm and steady hand, like a skittish horse who needs to feel her owner's control.

"Of course, you'd want to go first. You want to feel that pussy while it's tight, not stretched out."

"Fuck." The look of disgust Finn shoots Jack should whither him on the spot, but Jack smiles.

"I intend to, and so do you."

I'm about to respond when Skye appears in the doorway, dressed only in a shirt with its buttons mostly undone. She doesn't say a word but stares at each of us one by one before turning back and disappearing down the hall. My eyes meet Jack's, giving away my surprise. This girl isn't the nervous innocent I imagined. Maybe we won't need to break her in as much as I thought.

I'm the first to stride to Skye's designated room. The first to find her lying on the bed with her legs open and her hands by her sides. The shirt has fallen open, revealing white cotton panties and an upside-down V of pale skin across her belly, which glows in the soft light cast by the lamp on the nightstand.

Her eyes are fixed on the ceiling, her face impassive as she waits.

This isn't what I wanted. This isn't what any of us want. Maybe she's used to being used like a blow-up doll, or maybe she's clever in playing us at our own game.

Whatever the reason, the fantasy I constructed in my head is out of the window. I need to rethink what to do.

With Finn and Jack at my back, growing impatient now they're so close, I take a step forward, unbuttoning my shirt. Just the sight of her partially uncovered body has me burning with a fever. I toe off my work boots as I toss my discarded shirt onto the wooden chair Jack made last fall. I unhook my belt with one hand and pull it from the belt loops in a smooth movement. The loud whooshing sound makes Skye jump. My jeans drop to the floor, and I step out of them as I reach the bed. Skye doesn't look at me standing before her in just my black boxer briefs. She doesn't see the ink that covers my chest or the hunger in my eyes. She doesn't witness the flex of my hands at my sides as I decide what to do.

Disappointment swamps me, and it's backed up by something blacker and thicker. Bubbling resentment that even with all the planning and careful choosing, this isn't going to be what I need.

Well, maybe not tonight.

She's still and resigned, as though she knows she's not going to get anything from the physical process of sex and will just close her eyes and endure.

So, maybe the key to unlocking her is proving her wrong. I drop to my knees, grabbing her legs and hauling her ass to the edge of the bed. The rough action ruffles the blanket I spread over the sheets to keep her warm. Skye gasps but doesn't resist when I press my hot mouth over her panties and suck on her pussy. Even through the fabric, she smells warm and sweet, and something trips my brain like a switch being flicked. The possessive feeling ratchets up one hundred percent, and my fingers force her panties to the side, baring her tender pink flesh to me.

Skye doesn't resist when I slide my tongue from her sweet little opening to the bud of her clit. She doesn't whimper or move when I lap at her like the hungry dog I am. It's not until I push a thick finger inside her that she makes a sound. It's soft and breathy, and my cock kicks in response.

"That's it." Jack's low, growling voice cuts through the silence like the first rumble of a chainsaw. "That's it. Fuck that sweet pussy with your fingers."

Finn, who has undressed next to me, kneels on the bed and reaches out to touch Skye's hair. She closes her eyes, effectively shutting him out, and in response, I use the rough pad of my thumb to torture her sensitive flesh and shove two more fingers inside her, stretching her wide.

When her pussy clamps down on my fingers like a vice, I'm momentarily confused, but then the ripples start, and I know. She came with barely any effort, and the realization makes me crazy.

She's clean and on birth control. That was part of the contract. We were tested, too, so there's no need for condoms. All I have to do is shove down my underwear and climb between her slack thighs. When I loom over her, her eyes open, and their forest green shade feels as familiar as the trees outside my bedroom window. She blinks fast, as though her orgasm took her somewhere far away, and she's surprised to return to this unfamiliar place with us. I pull her underwear over her long, slim legs and take her hands in mine, forcing them to the bed next to her head. My cock notches at her entrance, and I hesitate, not because I don't want this, but because there is only ever going to be this one first time, and I want to prolong it.

"Just fuck her already," Jack barks, but I can't. Skye's lips part, and she looks like she wants to tell me something.

"What?" I ask her.

"I never had an orgasm before," she whispers.

And for the first time in a long time, I don't know what to say.

CHAPTER 3

SKYE

TWISTED INTO SUBMISSION

The lumberjack looming over me is huge compared to Carter. Over the past few years, I became used to my ex's lean body and accustomed to his size and weight.

This man is nothing like Carter.

West's chest is so broad, it obliterates everything behind him from my view. The swirling ink over his pecs, shoulders, and arms is so intense that barely any skin is visible. His belly is tight and firm, with a dusting of hair that runs down, down, down to the jut of a cock so big, I can't even fathom how he'll get it inside me.

But it's his face that I can't take my eyes off. Shorn dark hair peppered with silver makes him seem severe, and his eyes are dark and hard. Weathered, tanned skin stretches over a rugged masculine bone structure that shouldn't appeal to me, but it does. His lips are soft and glistening from the pleasure he gave to me. It's stupid, but

I want him to kiss me with that mouth.

This man is a stranger.

A stranger who wants to do things to me that only a lover should do.

Except the man who said he loved me proved to me time and time again that he didn't, and now the space between my thighs feels used up and disconnected from my mind and my body. Or rather, it did until West made stars flash behind my eyelids and heat swamp my brain until I was so overwhelmed I couldn't remember where I was.

He made me orgasm like it was as simple as flicking a light switch from off to on.

At my confession, he froze over me with wide eyes like I took a skewer and pushed it slowly into his heart.

Next to me, Finn's attention flicks between me and his friend, and Jack makes a low, growling, impatient sound.

For a moment, it's like my soul leaves my body, and I'm looking down at myself in this strange room that's more homely than the home I ran from. I'm surrounded by strange men who I dread less than the man who promised me the Earth and then forced me to stare into the depths of hell. Separated from myself like this, I can endure the violation of the cock poised to enter me. I can keep the breaths entering my lungs and hold the beat of my heart back from racing away.

Seconds tick by, and West seems torn. Then Jack mutters something about needing to step in to show West how it's done, and that's what brings West back into the room.

I'm wet between my legs, but the press of West's thick cock is still a violation that burns. He presses deep but moves slowly, proving himself more considerate than I expected, pulling back, and pushing forward, advancing inch by inch until I'm aching inside. Our bodies linked, I stare at his throat, where a tattooed spear points from his chest to his ear. I watch the thin skin flutter with his blood, the pulse faster than it should be.

He moves like the ocean, fucking into me in waves, his eyes fixed on my face. His hands, still braced around my wrists, are harsh, but his hips are liquid, swirling against me until I feel like I might break apart and be washed away, never to be found again.

"Fuck," he cries out, speeding as I come again like a whip cracking against ravaged flesh. I can't breathe. I can't think. I'm a body that's become separated from the mind that occupies it. I'm skin and bone and soft flesh torn open by this man who now owns me from my toes to the tips of my long, tangled hair.

Carter used to like to fuck me in front of a mirror, watching himself steal pleasure from my body. I didn't pretend to enjoy it and it never seemed to bother him. West looks directly into my eyes when he spills inside me, swelling and seizing, groaning with a release he seems to believe is not quite real. When he's done, he staggers back like he's been shot, releasing my wrists, bracing himself on legs that seem uncertain, his trunk of a chest heaving.

Finn, who's closest, bends over me, his blue eyes like the sky I used to stare into as a child when I'd spun myself into dizziness and fallen to the ground.

I'm dizzy now, too.

His sweet blond curls flop over his forehead, angelic almost.

"Skye."

I blink, wondering if it's a question or just an expression of some emotion he can't express.

When he bends to press his lips onto mine, I freeze, but his mouth is soft, and he takes the time to make the kiss teasing rather than invasive.

I spin like I'm drunk, telling myself to endure but finding myself slipping into pleasure that I don't know whether to greet or resist.

Finn's fingers fumble with the remaining buttons of my new shirt until they're released, and my breasts are bared to the room. His mouth moves to suck my nipples into stiff, wet points, sending electric sparking between my thighs. His hands discover all the softness I have, kneading and kneading as though I'm made of dough, and he wants to shape me into something that will please him. He hauls me onto his lap like I weigh nothing, pressing my body against the rock-hard plains of his chest. He smells of fir trees and cinnamon, of wood chips and winter, and he buries his face in my neck, inhaling my scent and moaning at the discovery.

It's easy to slide down onto his waiting cock. West has already spread me like butter and I'm dripping his cum. I don't need to move because Finn's bossy hands direct my movements, taking what he needs. Greedy fingers grab my ass, pulling me against the ridge of his pubic bone as he thrusts up into me like a jackhammer.

In his arms, I'm a wisp of a person. Insubstantial but necessary, out of control but bringing about the tumble of these men into utter weakness.

"You feel so fucking perfect," Finn gasps, and then his mouth finds mine, and his tongue slides inside, and I spin again.

This shouldn't feel good.

I told myself I could endure it for Hallie.

I told myself I could get through anything if I just kept my end goal in mind.

I imagined lying back and thinking of carefree days in my past or dreaming of carefree days in my future. I believed that I could be a passive participant in fulfilling the needs of my owners. But that isn't what this is, and I don't understand why.

"Skye." The sound of my name on Finn's lips cuts through all my confused thoughts. "Fuck, Skye."

And I come when he does, going slack in his arms as he slumps back against the plaid blanket, taking me with him.

"That's it. My turn." Jack hooks his arm around my

body, pulling me from Finn before our sweat has had time to cool. Finn's cock slips from inside me, and with it, liquid trickles, wet and warm, down the inside of my thigh. Like a rag doll, I'm pushed to the bed facedown. Jack's calloused hands grip my wrists together over my head, and he wraps them with warm leather, his belt or West's.

Panic surges through me, but I close my eyes and step outside my body when he tugs my hips up until I'm on my knees with my legs spread wide. His fingers probe roughly for his enjoyment, not mine, pumping in and out as though he wants to clean his friends from inside me. I grit my teeth, but then the pad of his middle finger finds my clit, and I almost scream. It's too swollen. Too sensitive. I can't take the pain of raw nerves and violent intrusion, except when he replaces his fingers with his cock, and enters me like a battering ram, I come so hard, I can't hold myself up. Instead, Jack supports my limp frame, hooking his huge branch of an arm beneath my stomach and holding my body exactly where he wants it until he, too, fills me to the brim.

Tears leak from my eyes, not because it hurts but because I can't hide the way any of these men have physically destroyed me and put me back together. Carter's pretense at emotion was so much worse than the indifference of these men. At least I know what they need and expect. If this is their worst, I know I can endure the year.

You like it. My internal whisper is both shocking and right.

I'm a masochist.

I'm disturbed.

I'm deranged for experiencing this pleasure, for not at least putting up some kind of fight.

And the reality is like a punch to the gut because I was never like this before Carter found me, and kept me, and broke me into a million pieces.

After, Jack stalks from the room. Finn unhooks the

belt from my wrist and pulls the blanket over me. West stands by the wall, his face in shadow, so I can't make out his expression.

Words hang in the air between us, but none are spoken for long, empty seconds.

"Sleep now." Finn climbs from the bed, lingering as though he's waiting for me to say goodnight.

When I remain silent, he follows West from the room, closing the door behind him.

I stare at the wall; rough plaster painted a shade of off-white. Unfamiliar shadows lurk in every corner, and I tug the blanket over my head, curling onto my side until I'm just a small lump beneath the fabric. Between my legs, the presence of the men outside this room lingers.

Tears burn my throat, but I won't shed them. I don't have the luxury of crying. No one cares if I'm happy or upset. No one will comfort me, so what's the point?

I try to sleep, but it remains elusive. Too much cortisol in my bloodstream. I don't want to be on high alert, but I am.

Eventually, I push the cover down and sit up. I pull the shirt closer around me and search the floor for my underwear, slipping from the mattress to retrieve the damp fabric from the floor. More cum leaks from inside me, and I press my legs together, not wanting to make a mess on the floor. I wipe myself clean with my panties as well as I can, then search for the bag that holds the items West purchased for me; it will make a temporary laundry hamper. I can wash them tomorrow by hand if that's all that's available. This cabin doesn't seem to be filled with modern appliances, but maybe I didn't notice them.

I didn't take in the room before, but now I find myself perplexed at the vase on the dresser and the soft pillows that decorate the bed. A rug on the hardwood floor runs down one side of the bed as though they were worried my feet would get cold when I woke in the morning. Things feel carefully placed, as though the three brutish lumberjacks wanted to make me feel at home.

It could have been Finn alone. Of all of them, he's the only one who touched me with any kind of care. I run my hands over the wooden chair in the corner, finding the surface smooth and warm. It's handmade, of that I'm certain. Beautiful craftsmanship that maybe one of the men here possesses.

The items West bought spread across the dresser, and I look at each one before folding and placing them into the top drawer. Everything looks like it will fit, which stuns me. How did a man with arms big enough to tear trees from the ground and a body like a bear know how to shop for a strange woman? Even the bralettes and panties he chose are the right fit. He bought me feminine hygiene products, even though he must have been embarrassed. The image of him standing in line with them makes me shake my head.

I drift to the closed door, pressing my ear against the smooth wood, straining to hear. The cabin is silent, each of the men having returned to their separate rooms, most probably. I listen and listen for so long that my ear hurts and my neck is strained. When I feel confident the coast is clear, I turn the handle tentatively, bracing myself for any noise that might wake them. It opens smoothly as though it's been recently oiled. A dim light emanates from the open-plan living area, and I walk slowly forward, searching the shadows, frantically trying to work out if I'm safe.

In the kitchen, I find an overturned glass by the sink and fill it slowly from the faucet, not caring if it's perfectly cold. I gulp down a full glass and then another, my thirst feeling unquenchable and my stomach completely hollow. The refrigerator stands tall to the right, and I stare at it, debating whether I should search for the food I desperately need. Just a slice of bread or a piece of cheese would get me through until morning. I place my hand on the handle, poised to open, when a low hiss cuts through the silence behind me.

"Looking for something in particular?"

I swivel, finding Jack looming close. He's wearing loose shorts which hang low on his hips revealing the insanely cut musculature of his chest and abs. His hair, which had been roughly fastened, is long and loose, hanging in waves that should look pretty but can't when he's so damned rugged. His lips are a mean line buried in his thick blond beard, and his arms hang at his sides, braced for some unknown fight.

He'd have no trouble tearing an average man limb from limb. I wouldn't stand a chance if he turned his coiled rage on me.

"I didn't eat today."

He breathes out through flared nostrils and strides forward. My flinch is instinct. I'm no stranger to harsh hands and violent words. The way Jack comes to an immediate halt at my reaction gives me pause.

Stepping back, he looks first at the ceiling and then at me. "Fix whatever you want, then get some sleep."

I watch his retreating form, the swagger of his long-legged gait, the sheer power in every prominent muscle stacked across his wide back. He's like Thor or an unknown Viking hero, stern and harsh but with incongruous boundaries that he won't cross. He saw my fear, and it changed him.

Quickly, I find bread, butter, and a small piece of cheese and fix myself a sandwich, which I take back to my room to eat.

I find my jeans and unfold the piece of floral cloth and the tiny photo inside. It's the only thing I brought with me. I bring the cloth to my nose and inhale. It doesn't smell of Hallie anymore, but I imagine that it does by looking at the picture and then closing my eyes with the image of her in my mind.

My heart is in two pieces: one that beats to keep me alive, the other that is held captive with all the love I used to feel trapped inside.

There's only one way to make it whole again. I must be patient and brave. As brave as Finn thinks I am. It's the only way to get through.

I wrap the photo again and slide it to the back of the drawer in the dresser, praying that nobody will bother to search it out.

Only then do I snuggle beneath the warm blanket and find the peace to sleep.

CHAPTER 4

FINN

DISARMED

I usually wake to the sounds of the forest. The gratitude I feel for these peaceful surroundings makes it easy for me to count my blessings. But this morning, I wake earlier than usual and breathe in the lingering smell of smoke that settles around the cabin overnight. The faint scent of coffee that overlays it is an indication that West is already up, starting the day in his usual way.

My immediate thought this morning is Skye.

I sit quickly, anxious to see how she is. Did she sleep well? Is she comfortable in the room we prepared for her, or is she scared and hesitant about what it will be like to live with us? I tried to make her room as welcoming as I could, but she must be nervous about being in an unfamiliar place with three unfamiliar men.

I dress quickly and step out into the hall, mindful of the familiar creaks of the wooden floorboards that could so easily wake someone who is sleeping lightly. As I predicted, West is brewing himself coffee so black, thick, and potent that you could stand a spoon in it. To my surprise, next to him and exaggerating his bulk is our new, petite house guest. She stands at the open fridge door, scanning its contents. Dressed in a nightshirt that I assume West picked out for her, Skye looks cozy yet exposed.

No one speaks.

West nods at me in greeting, and I do the same in return. We sit at the table while Skye busies herself.

In low voices, we exchange words. "How long has she been up?"

West lifts his shoulders and wrinkles his forehead. He doesn't know. Skye approaches, lowering hunks of bread spread with thick butter and jelly in front of us both. West likes a cooked breakfast, and I'm more of a cereal man, but neither of us objects.

"Thanks, Skye. How did you sleep?"

West almost chokes on his bread, coughing at its dryness. Swigging a huge mouthful of his coffee, he swallows hard and interjects.

"For Christ's sake, man. She's not a house guest."

Skye blinks. She drops her chin to her chest, crestfallen almost. When she clenches her hands into fists and inhales steadily before lifting her chin, it reminds me of last night, the tension and dejection followed by a determination to be brave.

She has grit.

"Have you eaten, Skye?" I won't let West intimidate me out of being a decent human being. She has to eat, for Christ's sake. She might not be our guest, but she's our responsibility. And she has just spent her first night with us.

She nods, and West shakes his head as if I'm a lost cause. It says more about him than it does about me, but I understand. It deviates from his expectations. Too much kindness crosses his fierce boundaries of restraint and control, and there is no place for it under the conditions of her contract.

It's what we agreed on and the only way I could convince Jack and West to go ahead with the arrangement.

We eat quickly, and I gulp down the coffee Skye pours me with milk and sugar, just how I like it. West shoves his chair back when we're done, scraping it loudly on the hardwood floor. "Jack is at the pack and load. Let's go!" He's right. It's time to get out there and join the crew.

"Can I come out with you?" Skye's voice sounds almost desperate. Is she frightened of staying here alone? I wouldn't blame her. The lodge is isolated, and the forest feels alive and strange if a person isn't used to it.

"Get dressed quickly, and we'll meet you out front." I wait for West to object, but he doesn't. Perhaps, he'll have her lugging logs around the yard if she really is only here to work and serve our needs.

Skye scuttles off, returning five minutes later in jeans, boots, and a blue plaid shirt over a white tank. She's scraped her hair into a high ponytail, which swings as she strides purposefully toward us. West's mouth drops open slightly but then he clears his throat and heads to the door.

Silently, we make our way along the path. I watch her soak in everything about the forest, her eyes bright and wide. West walks ahead of us, his big arms swinging at his sides with an air of detachment. He's my buddy—well, more like a brother—so I know he doesn't mean anything by it, but he's coming across as reserved and severe to Skye. I pull back to be next to her and enjoy seeing the forest through her fresh eyes. She's tiny amidst the mighty cedars that surround us.

She inhales deeply and slowly exhales in the same appreciative way I do, taking in the scents and the coolness of the shaded air.

I'm struck with the urge to take her hand in mine, but I don't because that's not what she's here for. She signed up for the money, not for a fake romance with an affection-starved lumberjack. I need to get it clear in my mind.

She's here to serve our needs.

So why do I feel so much like I want to scoop her up and keep her safe?

As if she senses my thoughts, she turns and smiles shyly at me.

Skye catches herself and quickly snaps her head away.

Her beauty is fragile almost, made up of delicate elfin features and pale skin. Her nose tips up at the end, and her rosebud lips are the same pink as a tiny flower that grows wild, their fullness giving her a sensual quality. Skye must feel me watching her because she turns towards me again and gives me another shy smile.

There is already a connection between us.

The gesture ignites a feeling deep inside me. Her vulnerability is clear even though she's working hard to put on a show of strength.

Why has she agreed to this contract? Maybe she's seeking a place of escape and a sense of peace here like the rest of us? More likely, it's all about the money.

The rumble of voices and machinery in the distance grows slowly closer, and we soon reach the clearing up ahead. I spot Jack over with the rest of the crew. He's usually the first up at the cabin and the first on-site. I'm not sure if he even sleeps half the time. His face is etched with exhaustion, which worries me. He visibly bristles when he lays eyes on Skye, his steely eyes narrowing with disapproval.

The men all turn when they see us approach, and I can't shake the image of a pack of hungry dogs as I raise my hand in greeting. Skye stops as if rooted to the floor. Does she sense it, too? The clear air suddenly takes on a tangible, thick feel, almost suffocating and clearly makes Skye feel uneasy. She shrinks back, waiting for me to pass so I'm in between her and the group. I keep her close.

"What kept you? Or do I even need to ask? Who's this beauty?" Nathan removes his hard hat and shakes out his shaggy hair. His eyes twinkle, but he's rough around the edges and must seem intimidating to Skye.

"Steady, bro! She's spoken for. And so are you, so get back in your cage." There is a rumble of laughter as Marcus adds his usual brand of humor to the moment.

Marcus and Nathan are brothers but like chalk and cheese.

"This ain't the time for ogling. We've got targets to hit today." Aiden is the oldest crew member and acts as deputy to Jack's Head Honcho, although it's all unofficial. He's a steadying presence, and I'm not sure what would happen without him.

Put together a group of testosterone-fueled men, and before you know it, a pecking order has formed.

And a pack mentality. It can have its advantages and disadvantages.

Ethan steps away from the group, and, in moments, his tall, lean frame is right on top of us.

"Protecting your prize, Finnie boy? Not gonna share the goods?" He lunges forward and grabs Skye by the arm, grazing her breast and tugging her towards him. His breath radiates the stale stench of liquor and tobacco, and I doubt he has showered in days. Why bother when you have to drive thirty minutes to the nearest bar for the very remote chance of female company?

Skye gasps and twists to break free from his aggressive grip and drops to her knees as he lets her go. Ethan laughs with a deep, menacing rumble, and I step forward without thinking, knocking him to the ground with one fist. I turn and offer my other hand out to Skye, who reaches in return so I can pull her to her feet. She turns away from the group, looking up at me, panic widening her eyes and tears threatening.

Jack breaks the silence.

"Get her out of here!" I don't need to be told twice.

I'm aware of Ethan ranting and raging behind us as we retreat. Jack steps in to deal with him, shouting something about keeping his hands to himself.

"Come on, boys. This isn't gonna get the work done, and I'm not hanging around for overtime today." Aiden steps in again as Skye and I retreat. He has a gift for smoothing Jack's rough edges, and it usually works.

Skye forges ahead of me, her head low and her shoulders hunched in a protective pose. She's a lonely figure, lost in the middle of trees that seem to stretch to touch the sky. I catch up to her and put my hand on her shoulder to slow her down.

"Thank you!" Her voice sounds choked as if she's trying not to cry. My protective instinct surges, but I'm afraid of crowding her, so I give her some space instead.

"You don't need to thank me."

We slow further still. I've read her well, and she faces me and offers me a tentative smile. Her eyes radiate sadness and fear. Red blotches swirl in angry patterns on her chest and neck, but as we continue to walk, she grows more relaxed. We fall into a slow step together, and I lead her into a familiar gathering of trees.

"What do you think of our forest?"

She tips her face, straining into the tree canopy. "Everything smells so good, so fresh."

"Yeah. The air is clear, not like the city."

"How long have you lived out here?"

I stop and rest against the rough bark of a thick trunk, bending my leg and resting my foot flat against the surface. "A few years."

Skye forces her hands into her pockets and chips at the fallen leaves with the toe of her boot. "It's so different from what I'm used to."

"When I came here, I felt the same. The silence was strange. And the darkness. Now, I'm grateful for the forest every day. I never take it for granted. It's a great place to bury your past and find a new future."

I hope it'll put her at ease, but she shakes her head as if she doesn't quite agree or as though she believes her past is too big and bad to bury anywhere. "You think you can bury your past?"

That's a good question, one I don't really know how to answer. "Maybe, if you distract yourself enough."

"Until you're not distracted anymore."

She's made a small circle before her, leaving rough brown earth exposed. "You're brave, you know...for doing this. I think you are anyway."

Again, a shrug and a shake of her head signal to me that she isn't on the same page. What is she thinking? What's so bad about her past that she doesn't believe she can outrun it? Why is she here?

"Are you always the positive one?" she asks, with a quick change of subject. "The one who keeps the peace?"

This catches me off guard. Is it so obvious in the short time that she has been here that this is the role that I have carved out for myself? The peacekeeper? "The others think I'm young and stupid. I tell them that you don't need to be an old man to learn life lessons. And you don't need to get bitter from learning."

Skye shivers, and I take off my jacket and wrap it carefully around her shoulders, and she pulls it closer. We are quiet for a few moments, but the air between us feels charged. I'm overwhelmed by the urge to pull her into my chest and soothe whatever is eating her inside, to kiss her deeply like I did last night, to lay her down and bring us both a distraction. My body still tingles at the memory of how it felt to be inside her. The orgasm we shared makes me feel as if we're connected.

Jack and West are right.

I'm foolish.

Imagining things that aren't there.

Wanting more from this than I'm ever going to get.

We walk again, reaching the clearing that I've been

leading us towards. When we stop, she gasps, pressing her hand to her mouth. We stand on the edge of a two-hundred-and-seventy-degree elevated crescent jutting outwards and are confronted with a valley so vast and expansive that it appears to have no end. With varying shades of winter green, burnt orange and a scattering of hardy brightly colored wildflowers thriving in the changing season that benefited from the glare of the sun and a break in the dense forest, it's beautiful enough to steal my breath.

A breeze rustles the trees nearby, and way off in the distance is the plaintive cry of a bird as it soars and circles on the hunt for its prey. The familiar rumbling of the powerful river cutting its way through the landscape around us draws her eyes.

"It's so beautiful," Skye gasps, her eyes flicking to mine before resting on the view again. We sit on the rocks nearby to take the weight from our feet. As the cascading water fills the silence between us, I think about what she said about not being able to bury the past.

"What made you sign up for the auction?"

She tucks a stray strand of hair behind her ear, staring into the distance. My mom had long, pretty hair like Skye's, and she used to do the same thing when the wind was strong. It's been a long time since I sat with a woman in the outdoors for nothing but conversation.

Skye swallows, her throat shifting to bury her truth. I can ask the question, but that doesn't mean she'll give me an answer.

Her desire for privacy stirs my protective instinct again. Whatever it is, I'm sure it's too painful for her to face. Whatever happened in her life before the auction is something I can't do anything about. All any of us can do now is try to make this year as good as possible.

"Money," she says eventually. "I did it for the money."

It's not the full story, of that I'm certain, but she doesn't know me, and she doesn't know my motives or those of Jack and West. I shouldn't expect her to open up so quickly.

But I can encourage her by being open myself. I don't have anything to hide from anyone. I'm not closed like West, and I don't wear my anger about life like a flaming shield like Jack.

"I always feel less alone out here. The trees, the birds, the clean mountain air. It's so different from where I grew up." I pause, trying to find the words to explain my history. "My mom died when I was thirteen. I ran away from the group home I was put into...I didn't have anywhere to go."

Skye studies me with a soft expression, which encourages me to go on. "Living on the streets was tough...always in the shadows, relying on the kindness of strangers. It taught me a lot about what's important, and I was lucky when Jack found me and gave me a chance."

"Jack did that?" Skye sounds surprised.

"He got me a job at the lumberyard and put a roof over my head."

She shakes her head like she can't quite believe that the man she met last night is the same good Samaritan I'm painting a picture of.

"I had a little sister, Carmel. She was only six years old when my mother died. She was quickly adopted, and there isn't a day where I don't wonder where she is."

Once again, I notice that Skye is clenching her fists, scoring grooves into her palms. I've said enough. She has an open wound; I'm sure of it.

I step to reach for her, putting an arm around her shoulder. She's stiff at first but then relaxes into my embrace. We stay like that for a while, then she turns, and her eyes search mine. There's longing in there, but I'm not sure what it is for. I lean in to kiss her sweet pink lips, and it's a warm and tender moment until we're interrupted by a skittish bird bursting forth from a tree branch nearby. She stands abruptly, rattled, and scans the wood for the source of the noise.

"It was only a bird." I try to reassure her, and she lets out a relieved burst of air.

"I feel like I'm trapped in a weird fairytale retelling of Goldilocks, except instead of bears, I've got lumberjacks."

"Oh yeah?"

"Yeah. Grizzly, Macho, and Kindheart." I snort with surprise because she's summed us up so easily. Her words are bittersweet because The Three Bears was the last book I shared with Carmel before we were separated. I linger on the memory for a moment and breathe in. This time, it's her turn to sweep me into an embrace. This woman senses my need, but as we close in together, I feel her body shaking, and I realize that she's sobbing silently into my shirt.

"Hey, it's okay." I smooth my hand over her back, pressing my lips to the warmth of her head. When her breathing calms, she draws back, staring into the distance as though she wants to put some space between us before she begins to need me too much.

"Let's go back to the cabin."

"I'll make some lunch," she says, and I nod.

We return the way we came to make the short journey through the trees to the lodge.

Moments pass in silence, and she still clearly has things on her mind.

After a few more paces, she turns to me. "Why does Jack hate me so much? I don't understand why he was at the auction when he doesn't want me around."

It's a difficult one to answer because I'm struggling to understand his motives myself. I can't confess to her what I think, that for him, it's a need for sexual control and something even darker. So, instead, I opt for something that may show Jack in a more favorable light and allow her to see him as I do.

"If it wasn't for Jack, who knows where I would be now. He's not a bad person." She nods slowly, absorbing this.

To my right, I notice a small cluster of purple wildflowers, and Skye watches me as I go over to where they are, bend down, and gather them into a small bunch.

"Here! For the vase in your room." A smile gathers at the corners of her mouth, and eventually, she relaxes enough to smile.

West and Jack aren't here to tell me I'm wrong for treating her like a woman, not a possession, and even if they were, I wouldn't care.

Seeing Skye smile is like watching the sun appear after an eclipse.

We continue, and in the distance, the cabin comes into view. As I watch Skye return to my home, I hope I've done enough to put her at ease about her time with us.

Before Jack and West have a chance to unsettle her all over again.

CHAPTER 5

WEST

LAYING DOWN THE LAW

I throw open the door to the lodge, expecting to find Finn and Skye sharing hot chocolate and baking cookies, but instead, I find Jack nursing a cup of coffee with the remnants of his lunch scattered on a plate he has shoved into the middle of the table. He glances up, setting his steely eyes on me, tipping his head once in greeting.

"Where's lover boy?"

Jack shrugs, but the deepening grooves between his brows reveal a mountain's worth of disapproval. "He's not here. No one's here."

I shake my head as I walk to the sink to fix myself a glass of water. This morning was difficult, not only because the physical labor was grueling but because Ethan was playing up. It happens every so often until someone's fist does everyone a favor and knocks him back into place.

Unfortunately, Finn's punch has the opposite effect.

I open the fridge, find the usual food, then scan the counters. "She didn't make lunch?"

Jack exhales roughly. "First day, and she's already shirking."

"Finn should have brought her back here immediately so she could clean up and prepare a meal."

"He should have, but he didn't."

I pour myself coffee, and even though my belly grumbles, I sit across from Jack.

"This is going to work," I say firmly. "There are bound to be teething problems. It's a new arrangement for all of us."

"There wouldn't be teething problems if people in this house weren't treating her like their new best friend."

"You know Finn. He's got a soft heart."

"Finn needs to rein it in. Otherwise, we're going to come to blows."

I raise my eyebrows sharply as Jack grits his teeth hard enough to make his jaw tick.

"No point in ruining a great relationship over a girl." It's a comment designed to lighten the atmosphere, but it doesn't.

"I said my piece on this already. I'm not going to repeat myself. Either you and Finn keep yourselves in check, or I will have to come down on her so much harder. At least one of us has to keep control."

"Everything's under control, Jack."

He sips his coffee and rests it on the table, slumping back in his chair. Silence stretches between us as I stare at the crumbs on Jack's plate, considering what to have for lunch.

"She did okay last night," he says eventually. "For the first time."

"She did," I agree, surprised at his compliment.

"If she straightens out about the rest, this could work out. But Finn needs to chill the fuck out."

"I'll talk to him."

Jack nods, reaching for his mug and downing the dregs. "But if she misses a meal, or I come home to the house looking shitty, she's going back."

I want to tell him that this house has looked shitty for the last five years, but I don't. No point in enraging the bear. And where would we return her to? If she had a home to go to, she would have come to us with some possessions. Maybe she wouldn't have needed to auction herself in the first place.

When Jack pushes back in his chair and presses his hands to the table surface, heaving up his bulk, I try to think through what I need to do to make Finn understand that he's putting the whole arrangement at risk and how I can make it clear to Skye what is expected. I rub my hand over my beard as Jack leaves the cabin.

I'm about to fix myself something to eat when there's a bang from somewhere in the cabin. Jumping up, I stride through the den and into the hallway, spotting Skye disappearing into her room. She's been here the whole time, and by the looks of it, she listened in to my conversation with Jack. If she heard anything, it puts us at a distinct disadvantage when it comes to control over this relationship.

Skye's about to shut the door when I approach and catch her stunned and fearful expression. I put my foot next to the doorframe, blocking her from closing it, but she doesn't even try. I fill the doorway like a huge slab of wood looming over her.

I don't need to say a word to make Skye tremble.

"Listening in on private conversations?"

"I didn't mean to. I was…"

I put my hand up, silencing her immediately. "There are two things you need to know about me, Skye. I don't like liars, and I don't like excuses."

Her skin blanches, and she shrinks back a step. "I was going to tell you I was here, but then I heard you talking about me, and I thought you'd be angry if I interrupted."

"I'm angry now." I lean into the room, supporting myself on one arm braced on the door jamb, stretching out my tired muscles. "Finn isn't doing you any favors by treating you like you're his girlfriend. He can't help himself, though. He's just a good person, through and through. But me and Jack... we're not so good." My words drop like lead between us, and her lips part on unspoken words. "The contract makes it clear what we expect for our investment. I suggest you read it and take it in. Be careful not to make Finn think that he's anything more to you than he is. Jack is Jack. If you do what he says, this arrangement will last the year."

She blinks, and I allow my gaze to trail over her body, finding red blotches peppering the skin over her chest and neck.

"And you?" she asks.

"What you see is what you get." It's not that simple. Life never is. But it's all I've got to give.

"I'll read the contract."

I nod, slicking my tongue over my teeth. "Don't miss mealtimes. Keep the place clean. And at night, don't lock this door."

There are a lot more stipulations in the contract, but she can research those herself.

"Okay."

"What happened at the lumberyard today..."

Skye nods, shrinking back another step.

"It wasn't your fault. Ethan isn't a good guy. He doesn't like me, and he took it out on you."

"Why doesn't he like you?"

The question is the wrong one. She doesn't have the right to dig around in my past. This is exactly what Jack was talking about and exactly what I need to put a stop to. I step into the room, putting myself within touching distance of the pretty girl in front of me. I reach out, cupping the side of her neck, resting my thumb against her windpipe, and pressing just enough to trigger her to swallow. "Don't ask questions, pretty girl. You might not like the answers."

Skye's frozen, with wide green eyes that stare up at me, clouded with fear. Her chest heaves with a long shaky breath, and in my filthy work jeans, my cock stirs.

I have time for lunch or sex.

I like a sandwich as much as the next man, but not enough to leave this room, no matter how hollow my stomach feels.

"Get on your knees, Skye." My voice is a husky, gravelly baritone that rumbles in the silence of the lodge.

Skye obeys immediately, pressing her hands flat to the wooden floor and staring straight ahead at my thighs. I slip the end of my belt out of the metal buckle and flick my jeans open with well-practiced speed. Pulling my cock from my jeans is easy, and Skye looks at my thick meat like it's a club I'm about to kill her with. I stroke it up and down with tight, firm, almost painful strokes while she watches with wide eyes. "Open that sweet mouth," I demand as I rest my palm against her cheek, running my thumb across her pink lips. Her eyelids drop closed as she exhales, then she opens up; and I paint her bottom lip with my precum before forcing my cock between her lips. She sucks me like the good girl she is with technique she must have learned at the hands of another man.

Possessiveness is an emotion I didn't know I could feel, but I do. This girl at my feet is mine, and the idea that anyone else has or will touch her is flaming rage in my belly. The memory of Ethan pawing Skye rushes through my mind, and I have to close my eyes so that I can focus on the feel of her silky mouth and rough tongue on my dick and not how much I want to kill him.

"That's it," I croon, touching her cheek and urging her faster with a quick tug at the back of her neck. Her hands brace against my knees as she swallows me down. Her eyes leak tears, but she doesn't stop.

"Touch yourself," I tell her. She blinks, surprised, but

does what I ask, snaking her hands down the front of her jeans. "That's it. Touch that sweet pussy. Make it drip for me."

Skye moans around my cock, and the vibrations tickle over my balls. I grit my teeth. I'm so close that the pulsing heat at the back of my spine surges, and then she swallows and swallows, and all I can do is look down at her as she takes everything I have to give and pray that my legs don't go out from under me.

When she lets my dick slip from between her lips, I tuck it back inside my jeans, fastening the zipper, button, and then my belt. Her hand in her jeans stills, but I'm not letting her off the hook. Sex should never be a one-way street, even when you're paying for it.

"Get on the bed, Skye."

She scrambles to her feet, obeying my order so quickly and perfectly that my spent cock twitches again. I'm over her, unzipping her jeans and tugging them over her legs so fast she gasps.

When I spread her legs, dipping down to taste her, I find her pussy slick with arousal.

Fuck.

She really got off on blowing me. There's no hiding how much she likes it.

And when I lick her through her sweet labia, up and over her clit, she comes with jerky movements that look more like an exorcism than an orgasm.

I can't take my eyes off her. The total surrender. It's intoxicating. Even though Skye is obviously far from innocent, there's an unworldliness about her that brings out my protective instincts like a flash flood. I shouldn't lay next to her and gather her into my arms, but I do.

This is exactly what I warned Finn about, but I don't care. It feels too good.

Skye seems surprised but snuggles against my work shirt, grabbing a handful of the buttons at the center. She breathes fast and hard against my chest, her body taking minutes to reach equilibrium, and I feel the same.

The clock is ticking, and I need to get back to work, but even when her breathing is normal, she doesn't pull away from me as I expect, and while she still snuggles up against me, I can't find the will to be the first to move.

"Was it good?" she asks me eventually. "Did I do good?"

I jerk to look down at her, but her eyes are hidden by lowered lids.

"It was good, Skye."

She exhales gently.

"Was it good for you?" I find myself asking.

"Yes. I…" she pauses, tipping her face up to me. "…you make it so easy."

There's awe in her voice and shyness. She seems not to understand her pleasure or my ability to give it. I want to tell her that it's not just me who controls it. There's something inside her mind that finds our interactions arousing enough to trip her switch so easily. A secret fantasy. Something darker than she knew she liked.

If she found it harder, I'd persevere until I beat the block, but I'm thankful I don't have to.

Skye's quiet again, but I practically hear her brain whirring over questions. I play with her hair, letting the silky strands flow through my fingers over and over in a way that mesmerizes me. She shifts, and out of instinct, I tug her bare leg up and over my body so she's half laying over me, her spread sex opening against my rough jeans. She shifts with a small movement that must feel good. Is she hungry for more?

Jack was worried this arrangement wouldn't work out because she'd find our requirements too difficult and our physical needs too demanding, but that doesn't seem to be the case at all.

"What do your tattoos mean?" she asks me, pressing her hand against my chest where she knows they swirl like an angry riot of black and color.

"Different things," I answer. "Memories from my past."

"You were in the military?"

I jerk like she kicked me. What does she know about that?

"Yeah," I say, but I don't give away anything else. Talking about my service brings back the memories I came to this forest to bury. The man I used to be is not a man Skye would want to lay in bed with. I should warn her that dragging up old memories can haul the ghosts with them, but she's so young. What does she know about ghosts, memories, and hardship?

Maybe more than you think. She's here, isn't she?

Before she has a chance to respond, I ease her away from me and slide my legs off the edge of the bed. I'm hard as a rock and have to adjust myself as I stand to leave the room.

"Make steaks for dinner," I say. "With fries. It's Jack's favorite meal."

I don't look back to see if she heard.

Back at the yard, I find Jack in deep conversation with Finn. My friends are both giants of men, but beneath the trees that stretch to the gods, they seem tiny and insubstantial.

"I talked to her." Their conversation stops when they hear my voice. "She understands what to expect from us and what we expect from her. There shouldn't be any other problems."

Jack nods, and Finn grimaces.

Over Jack's shoulder, I spot Ethan cutting a narrow-eyed glance in our direction. He smiles with a curl to his lips, and rage whips through me. Rage and shame.

"I warned him off," Jack says, reading my mind.

"And he listened?"

"The man has a screw loose and lacks the brain cells that he needs to function like a normal person. Who the fuck knows?"

Finn glances over at Ethan, then at me. His eyes are sympathetic in a way that claws at me. "He's wrong, you know."

I stalk away before I get dragged into another conversation that won't do anything to change my mind about what happened. Ethan is and always will be a thorn in my side and a reminder of my weakness.

It's my cross to bear, and I don't need anyone trying to make it easier.

CHAPTER 6

JACK

HARD LESSONS

I ache like hell from a hard day's graft in the yard. My stomach is growling like a hungry wolf, and my temper is frayed. This thing between Ethan and West is getting out of hand. Targets need to be met, and it only takes one link in the chain for it to go to shit. Ron Maggs is the financial clout behind this yard, and he tasked me with the manpower management a few years back. I don't have the patience for Ethan's bullshit. My jaw clenches at thoughts of Ron's sweaty face, smug expression, and huge belly. I'll need a pay raise if I'm expected to manage staff tantrums, too. I'm not a fucking therapist.

And Skye and Finn hanging out like high school sweethearts is another itch to scratch.

I'm not the type to run off my tension but I need to do something.

I watch the crew as they gradually leave the site, making

their way to their trucks and back to whatever keeps them in place. Most of the time, that's Reggie's bar. I pack away everything valuable and lock up the yard in my own brooding company. When I'm done, I make my way home.

Home.

Seems a funny word for a cabin in a forest shared with two other men, but it is what it is. West is convinced Skye is going to make our place more homely, but I'm not so sure. Where it used to be somewhere for me to relax, now I feel on edge, and she plays Finn like a fucking banjo. I know that much.

I want to know more about why she's with us. I don't trust her as far as I can throw her.

Approaching the cabin, I catch a waft of flame-grilled meat in the air. My stomach growls again as I imagine a nice T-Bone, rare, smothered in butter and washed down with something home-brewed.

Nice idea. Must be my mind playing tricks on me.

Grabbing West's tomahawk from the porch, I go around the back of the cabin. The ax is just the right weight, swings like a motherfucker, and makes me feel like the king of the world. Despite my uncomfortable shoulder, I smash the thick logs into splinters, driven by the relentless rage that bubbles inside me every waking moment. It's only suppressed when I'm busy or forced to shove it down so that I can interact like a normal human being.

I should focus on making something again, instead of destroying. The table in the kitchen has served our cabin for many years and took all the best parts of me to make. The craftsmanship is something I should let myself be proud of. But pride is a waste of time. It's a notion for hopeful fools.

The rocking chair in Skye's room is another one of my projects. Was it too kind a gesture to leave it for her? My grandmother used to sit in her rocking chair and knit. She always seemed peaceful when she did.

Are we making her feel too comfortable here?

Damn Finn, talking me around with his thoughtful suggestions before Skye arrived. *Women need small gestures and tokens to make them feel appreciated.* I grimace at the thought. I don't give a crap what women need.

There hasn't been a single woman in my life who's given a crap about me.

My frenzy momentarily intensifies as the discomfort in my chafed palms, worsens with every swing.

Sweat drips from my brow and falls into the dust and dirt, and Finn comes into view. He's a lumbering bull of a man. A giant with the heart of a marshmallow and eyes pretty enough to make a damsel in distress out of even the hardest woman.

"Dinner's ready. You gonna join us? Think you should!" Finn looks hopeful.

I'm a sweaty mess but as ravenous as a bear right out of hibernation. And probably as pissed off.

When I follow him around to the front door and step inside the cabin, I'm struck by the sound of laughter. *Are they telling jokes?* My stomach lurches, and my pulse quickens. Skye wears an unbuttoned shirt, which looks like one of Finn's, and some loose pants, which reveal a flash of her milk-white stomach as they hang around her hip bones like an invitation. Her eyes follow me across the room, and the corners of her mouth tip up hopefully. I don't reciprocate the gesture, but I do imagine sliding my hands up her pale, exposed thighs after I've ripped off those pants with one sharp tug. My cock stirs and stiffens. Pulsing heat from the fire hits me hard, and I loosen my sweat-soaked shirt.

"I'll have a coffee." My gaze roots her to the spot, but I jerk my head, and she immediately scuttles off. Perhaps we're beginning to understand each other.

Finn stiffens in my periphery; he disapproves of my tone. Too bad. It's a firm message.

Both he and West are clean, fresh, and ready for

something. The atmosphere is relaxed, and I'm here disturbing the peace.

West raises his bulk from the table and slaps me across the shoulder in an attempt at camaraderie. I straighten myself up, but my eyes travel back to Skye.

"I haven't got all day!" Growling, I fail to keep a lid on my brewing frustration.

I'm conflicted.

I want her to tend to our needs, but how comfortable do I want *her* to feel in *our* space?

West interjects, snapping me out of the moment. "Bloody hard grind today. Let's have something stronger." He lumbers over to the unit in the corner that I carved last year and reaches in for the Jack Daniels. Skye appears at my side, her body heat radiating tangibly through her flushed cheeks and patchy red chest. Is she scared or just not used to working so hard?

"I have a bottle of red here. I found it in the pantry. It could go nicely with the steaks?"

Skye gingerly extends a dark and slightly dusty glass bottle, trembling almost imperceptibly with nervous energy. She smells of something sweet and lingering, which stays suspended in the air after she returns to the grill. She sounds so desperate to please that I almost feel sorry for her. I grip the back of my neck and shoulders, which have now seized up, as ripples of pain seer through my upper body and down my arms. Three sets of eyes are trained on me now.

Am I that much of an ass that everyone wants to see how I will respond to Skye's wine gesture?

She's not getting around me that easily.

Maybe, if she has made fries to accompany the meat, I'll show her my appreciation later. A sly smile twists my lips.

"You gonna set the table, Skye?" West's deep and husky voice carries across the room. Finn looks over at him in surprise. And something else. Skye's bottom lip wobbles.

West has the bottle of Jack pressed under one arm and three tumblers wedged between his thick fingers. With his free arm, he pokes the hearth, which releases a satisfying groan and a burst of heat. I stare into the flames that share the intensity of my own simmering rage, lurking like bright orange cinders at the back of my throat and deep in my core.

The heat and intensity are the same.

Perhaps West's idea isn't so bad. I anticipate the quick fix of a shot burning the back of my throat. He isn't including Skye in his gesture. It's her and us. *He* at least recognizes that.

Skye stands at the griddle, turning four huge steaks that she doesn't struggle to handle. I salivate at the smell radiating from the heat of the meat, and I focus on my foot as it taps against the wooden floorboards. Finn's silence feels strangely loud, but I avoid his gaze. I'm not sure how to play this. It's his fault that she wasn't here earlier to prepare lunch because he had her playing Hansel and Gretel in the forest.

"How do you all like your beef?"

West places a shot glass in front of me, and I down its contents. I exhale sharply and twist my neck in appreciation of the burning sensation as it shoots down the back of my throat. The bones in my spine crack audibly.

"I like mine dripping blood."

Skye nods as if in agreement, keeping her eyes cast low. West refills my shot glass.

We both down it in one gulp before West responds. "It will be good when you know what we like and don't have to ask. I like mine well done, so you've got to get the timing right."

West seems to have listened to me earlier, at least. Finn leans in to pick up the wine bottle to fill the glasses. My eyes tell him to sit back down. It's *her* job to pour the wine and *our* job to relax and enjoy.

Skye struggles under the weight of the huge, loaded plates as she lays them on the table. We all inhale, lingering on the smell. There hasn't been something quite this good served at the table in a long while, if ever. West's attempts at serving a meal are reflective of his military mindset, portion-controlled basics. Finn will do something that requires as little cooking as possible. He would have us live on cereal and potato chips if he could. I'm tired of being the only one who can throw together a decent meal around here. But this plate here suggests that I can hang up my imaginary apron. I inhale the steam as it rises off the perfectly done fries; she has cooked the steak exactly how I like it.

I don't want her to sense my approval, though. I can't help myself. "Anything green to go with this?"

Skye freezes. Her neck is a swirl of red blotches, and her hand travels to her cheek. *Is she feeling the heat or buying herself some time?*

"Um, I didn't find anything in the pantry."

Casting a look at Finn, she's clearly hoping for some moral support. He says nothing and fixes his gaze on his plate.

I enjoy the slightly salty taste as the meat melts on my tongue. Hacking off another huge chunk, I focus on the juiciness and flavor before chewing and swallowing. Not much chewing required. Skye has done a damn good job, and it's obvious from the appreciative moans from the other two that they feel the same.

We could get used to this.

I steal a look at Skye. Her delicate throat contracts as she swallows, the redness receding slightly. My cock stirs in my pants, even at this simple action of watching her eat. She catches my gaze, and we lock eyes as she reaches for her wine glass and takes a gulp, leaving a red stain on her lips that she doesn't wipe away with her napkin. My pants start to feel tighter as my thickening cock takes up any available space. I cough to clear my throat and try to push away an increasing urge swelling inside me.

Food first.

Sexual gratification later.

The noises of enthusiastic chewing fill the cabin. No one says much tonight. It's as if everyone is holding their breath, but the air is charged even without conversation.

There is now only a faint glow from the fire, which casts an almost celestial halo around Skye's head. Her hair is tied into a loose ponytail, which sits on one side of her face and rests gently over her shoulder. The skin of her cheeks is luminescent.

My mind is foggy with all the things I want do to her.

What is going on in her pretty little head?

I squash the urge to compliment her on her cooking and instead watch her fingers gripping her cutlery. The juice from her steak drips onto her fingers somehow, and she's trying to stop her knife and fork from slipping from her grasp. Sensing my eyes on her again, she puts her cutlery down and her words sound awkward in the already stilted atmosphere.

"I'm sorry about today. I shouldn't have asked to come to the site with West and Finn. It caused a problem and…" She trails off as though she's not sure what else to say. West's cutlery smashes onto his plate. The mention of anything to do with Ethan is not welcome around this table. But I'm not in the mood to consider his feelings about the matter. He clutches his collar and loosens his shirt as if trying to release the tension bursting from behind the buttons.

"I don't want to cause any problems while I'm here." She's trying too hard. She doesn't realize that it wasn't about her. She was just a pawn in Ethan's game. "Can I run you a bath after dinner, Jack? I found some eucalyptus earlier in the bathroom cabinet. I wonder if you'd feel better soaking your muscles…you look like you're in pain."

Too much. She's trying too hard. Her words sound as fake and bright as my mom's used to after I crept out of my room, bruised, and battered after one of my stepfather's rages. Like fixing me a shitty meal could make up for turning her eyes away from my pain.

I ignore Skye's comment. I just want to eat my goddamn steak in peace.

Finn and West have cleared their plates of every scrap of food, and West wipes up the remnants with a chunk of bread like a vulture devouring roadkill.

Finn gets to his feet, leaning over to pick up Skye's plate. "That was absolutely incredi-…"

I can't help it. I erupt, even surprising myself. Banging my fist down hard on the table, I rise to my feet, my chair toppling backward and crashing down to the floor. A roar forms in the back of my throat. "For fuck's sake, god damn it, Finn! How many times have I got to remind you that she's not some girl you have taken around to impress your damn parents." I've touched a nerve. Finn's shoulders raise, and he slumps back down at the table, but, in a split second, he's on his feet again, and this time, he's leaning over in my direction, drawing back a huge, meaty fist.

Before it can make contact with my face, West is in between us fast. The ligament in his thick neck is tight, and beads of sweat gather at his temples. I sense the formidable power he must have relied upon during his time in the military.

"Way too much, Jack!" Finn speaks, but his words sound choked with emotion. It was not a good thing to say to an orphan, but helping Skye with house chores is directly calling our arrangement into question once again. He disregards my opinion over and over.

A pitiful sound pierces the air. Skye has her hands over her ears, and her eyes scrunched tightly shut. She's braced so still, it's like she isn't breathing at all.

Pity trickles down my throat and into my chest, but it

only makes me angrier. Women know how to manipulate men. It's in their DNA. She's trying to make me feel sorry for her, so she'll have an easy year. If she has her way, Finn will wait on her hand and foot, and West will have his face permanently between her thighs. She'll be calling the shots. Of that, I'm sure.

I decided a long time ago that I would never let a woman under my skin, and I intend to keep my promise.

"If this shit carries on, she's out of here. Do you understand? We already have one stray dog under this roof. We don't need another."

The words are out, rippling around the bare-beamed room like a clap of angry thunder before I've had a chance to think about their impact. My tongue stings as Finn's cheeks flash red, and he turns his back on me without a second thought and lumbers over to Skye. West appears momentarily stunned into silence, heaving in his huge chest and exhaling loudly.

"Oh man, even for you, that was low!" He stands stock still, watching me, his eyes portraying something I can't figure out.

Is that pity or hatred?

My heart hammers in my chest as I turn to face the porch for my escape, but instead, I storm in the direction of my room. In my haste, my thigh catches one of the table legs, and Skye's glass, which must have been dangerously close to the edge and still full, tumbles to the floor. I carry on going despite the sound of shattered glass and the splash of the blood-red wine as it splatters to the ground.

Slamming my bedroom door with a force that vibrates the walls, I glance at my appearance in the mirror hanging over the dresser. I'm a disheveled wreck of a man, and my eyes are wild and crazy, as sharp, and dangerous as the glass on the kitchen floor. The smell of sweat sticking to my body cloys in the back of my throat, and I rip open my shirt so fast that buttons bounce off the floorboards. My erratic breathing makes my head spin, and I throw open the window, letting in a rush of icy frigid air that slaps me around the face and makes me shudder.

The sounds and scent of the forest are no comfort.

I kick off my boots and peel off my socks, and on autopilot, I strip the rest of my clothes from my weary body and head to the shower.

The warm water does nothing to soothe me. Dirt and sweat wash from my hair and skin, but the thick black feeling wedged inside me stays put. I press my palms against the cool tiles, letting the steaming water run over my face, holding my breath longer than is comfortable.

This is why I didn't want a woman here. One-night stands are one thing, but someone around all the time, getting under my skin is just too fucking much.

Skye's just too sweet, and it's sickly. Fake. It reminds me too much of the past when I felt helpless.

I swipe at my face, angry that I let my emotions out, even in rage.

It's as much of a display of weakness as Finn's kindness.

I can't allow it to happen again.

When I'm done, I use my worn, rough towel to dry myself, and then I throw myself down on the bed, which creaks and moans under my weight.

I should go right back out there and drag her in here. She needs to learn what it takes to be a woman in this house. I'm not scared of West's or Finn's disapproval, but I did overstep the mark. I need to chill the fuck out before I give myself a stroke.

My hand finds my cock, and I lay back, letting my knees drop and slacken. Using my precum as lubrication, I circle my thumb around the head of my erection, and as my lids flicker, I move my gaze to the window and then over towards the mirror. The height of it allows me to tip my face out of the scene so that I don't have to look into my own eyes. I have the choice of looking down at my throbbing cock as I grip and pull firmer and faster, but I decide to watch my reflection as if I'm detached from myself.

I see a powerful man with a huge handful of raw energy. My arm muscles are tight, and my forearms grip with obscene strength. While I'm doing this, I feel numb inside. I can chase away the memories that haunt me.

This is what Skye was supposed to do for me. Before she arrived, I imagined being able to inflict my desires on her, extracting a deep, dark, and all-consuming release.

But here I am, jacking myself off until I come into my fist, swallowing my moans, and resenting the desperate sounds of my ragged breaths. Hating my own fucking surrender.

The ache in my upper body returns, penetrating me to the core. Cool air gusts through the room, chilling my wet hand. I reach for my shirt to clean myself up and toss it into the hamper. Skye can deal with that tomorrow.

The power goes suddenly, sending the room into a blinding darkness, and I grab the torch from the top of the nightstand where I always keep it and fumble about for matches and the candle from my closet. As I watch the flame grow and flicker, my reflection in the mirror looks even wilder.

I head over to the window and pull it firmly shut, silencing the rustling of wind in the trees. There is a muffled sound as I return to my bed to sit down, then a light tap on the door.

"Come in."

The door moves, opening just a crack. Finn and West would have knocked loudly before opening the door, so this is neither of them. This is Skye, too scared to come right in. She hovers in the doorway like Red Riding Hood, catching sight of the wolf in her grandmother's bed. My cock stirs again as her gaze sweeps over my naked body. I take a breath and shudder. Exhaling, I grin.

Maybe I will get what I hoped for tonight, and if I do, Skye will learn what it takes to be a woman in my house.

CHAPTER 7

SKYE

AN AX TO GRIND

"You need to go to him," West tells me as he helps me pick up the shattered glass and wipe the spilled wine. "You need to prove to him that you're not scared of him and that he can rely on you for what he needs."

"And what's that?" I ask.

"Someone who doesn't expect anything but is prepared to give everything."

My eyes widen with surprise. That sounds like a thankless role to have in anyone's life, but it's one I've been used to providing for years. Carter is a man just like that. One with no conscience or emotional core. One who can use and abuse other people without a shred of remorse. I can't believe I escaped him and have fallen into another situation with a man just like him.

"I can't," I whisper.

"You have to." West's eyes are soft, but his words are

harsh. He rises from his crouched position, tipping the glass into the trash with a jangle. "Leave it for a while. Clear up. Take some time to calm down. Then go to him."

When I rise, my legs feel weak, and I grip the edge of the table to stabilize myself. West focuses on the whiteness of my knuckles. "He's not a bad man, Skye. Just a troubled one."

The same thing can't be said for Carter, even by his so-called friends. People only hang out with him for what he can do for them, not for who he is. Even though the men in this house have been coming to blows with each other, I can tell there is a deep-rooted friendship beneath it all.

"Will he hurt me?" I ask.

"Maybe." Finn makes a scowling sound from behind me, and West shoots him a disapproving look. "But it's never about revenge, Skye. It's always about control and pleasure. It's about those dark places that lurk at the edges of desire."

I shudder, understanding what West means. Sex isn't flowers and roses for most people. It's a way to find a release for our troubled souls and control in an out-of-control world.

It's been something that I've mostly pretended to like to please Carter. When I thought he loved me, I made allowances for the fact he was a selfish lover. When I realized he didn't have even a shred of feeling for me, it became something I endured.

Do I now have to endure it the same way with Jack?

He made you come, my internal voice whispers. And he achieved it by doing things to me that I would never have thought I would enjoy.

He might do it again.

The reality is that I don't have a choice, whether it's pleasurable or not. I have to find a way to keep this man happy or I won't get the money I need.

I glance at Finn and find him sitting with his head hanging. West barks his name, and they both leave the room, pausing in the hallway to the bedrooms to argue in whispered tones.

The plates are already clear of food, so all I have to do is wash them and leave them to drain. The pans are harder to clean, but the motion of scrubbing is cathartic. All the while, my heart races in my chest at what faces me after I'm done making the cabin presentable.

I check the pantry and fridge and find a pen and paper to jot down the food items that I need to keep the kitchen running. In the cupboard beneath the sink, I find a limited supply of cleaning products, so I add a few more items to the list. Maybe one of the lumberjacks will take me to the nearest store, and I can pick things out for myself. The prospect of doing something so mundane gives me a glimmer of something to look forward to outside of these four walls.

The house is quiet by the time I'm finished, and I pad softly into the hallway, listening out for any sign of life. My heart beats so fast against my ribs that I have to place my hand over my shirt to contain it.

I need to do this.

But confronting Jack is like facing Carter all over again.

I can't bring myself to knock on the door but stand frozen like a statue instead.

Maybe I should let him come to me. I can leave my door open like they insisted and see who decides to use my body tonight.

But that isn't what West instructed, and I can't disobey because I'm already treading on thin ice.

I raise my hand to knock on the door, but before I can, all the lights in the cabin flicker and then go out. The darkness is so deep and ominous, I gasp. I wave my hand in front of my face, but I can't see a thing. This deep in the forest, there is no light, and even the moon tonight is just a thin mocking arc in the sky.

In a panic, I knock softly on Jack's door. Somehow, the wolf inside seems less daunting than the dark emptiness outside his room.

His voice barks for me to enter, so I do, finding a soft flickering candle casting dancing shadows in the room and a very naked Jack sitting on the edge of a large wooden-framed bed.

In the low light, he's like a crouching giant, ready to unfurl his might.

"The lights went off," I whisper.

"Close the door."

He stands, making no effort to conceal his huge and very hard cock. It taps his navel as he takes a step closer, using two fingers to beckon me in a gesture that seems completely explicit.

Like he's pulling strings connected to my body, I move closer. The scent of him is everywhere: woodsy with a hint of citrus, and underneath, something masculine that is uniquely him.

He's showered away the filth of the day, but I can't forget the scent of his sweat that lingered in the kitchen after he left, like a drug that clouds my mind, making me forget how harsh and terrifying he is.

His eyes narrow, assessing me. The tangle of his dirty-blond hair surrounds his face like a lion's mane. Deep in his beard, his lips form a grim line.

"What are you here for?"

I blanch, embarrassed to answer. Still, I push to find the courage. "For whatever you need."

"Whatever I need...?"

He's close enough to touch me, but he doesn't. Instead, he looms over me, his impossibly broad chest like a living wall. I drop my lids, needing the safety of the darkness behind them. Jack takes my hand and, with harsh fingers, wraps my palm around his cock. "You feel this?"

I nod, my mouth so dry I can barely swallow.

"You're going to take this, Skye. You're going to take it whether you want to or not, but in the end, you'll beg for it."

His other hand cups my pussy, hard enough that he lifts me onto my toes. "This is mine. Do you understand me? Mine to touch. Mine to taste. Mine to use."

It's the word *use* that causes a hot pulse of heat to clench my internal muscles.

Why do I find the baseness of his actions and the harshness of his words arousing? West told me I have something in me that enjoys the way they are. Maybe he's right.

"Take off your clothes and get on the bed." Jack squeezes my wrist, and I let go of his cock, fumbling to strip away Finn's shirt and my tank, shoving my pants and underwear over my hips. I don't look at Jack, but I feel his burning gaze on me as I climb onto the bed and lay on my back.

I expect him to flip me onto my front like last time. I expect the same remoteness he fucked me with when West and Finn were in the room, but I'm wrong to make assumptions.

So very wrong.

He returns from his dresser with lengths of rope in his hands, and I lay frozen, knowing what's coming next and completely powerless to do anything to stop it.

You need to prove to him that you're not scared of him. West's words linger at the edges of my mind. I've had years of pretending not to be terrified. Years of plastering a smile onto my face and concealing the tremble of my hands.

Jack is cold and ruthless, but Carter was worse.

Carter was a cold-hearted killer.

Jack's face is impassive as he ties my left wrist to the left corner of his bed. He slowly and methodically does the same thing with my right. He eyes my feet but must decide that he wants them free, at least for now.

Even though it's futile, I test the ropes, finding them secure.

I tell myself that if Jack goes too far, West and Finn will come for me. They'll stop Jack if he loses control.

There's no sign that he will, though—just the eerie coolness of a man eyeing property and deciding what to do with it.

I keep my legs pressed together and bent slightly. When Jack rounds the end of the bed, I anticipate him forcing them open, but he doesn't. Instead, he pushes my lower body to one side so my bent legs are pressed into his comforter. He runs his hand over my exposed hip and ass with gentle strokes that feel strange coming from him. He lulls me into a trance-like state with his calloused palm, and I close my eyes, wondering how he wants to do this to me when there are so many other options. Then, without warning, his hand slaps my ass so hard, I cry out.

The burning wave of pain takes my breath away, but then Jack rests his big palm against my ravaged flesh, calming the sensation. My eyes meet his in the flickering yellow light, and there's no excitement in their depths. There's just a cold calculation where a soul should be.

He spanks me again, this time even harder, and I whimper as he rests his thumb against my asshole and presses rhythmically. I clench against any intrusion, but he doesn't stop, and a strange warm feeling of arousal tickles over my clit and pools low in my belly.

Again, the weight of his palm stings my skin.

By now, I must wear his handprint on my ass, but the pain diminishes more quickly, leaving liquid heat in its place. His fingers penetrate my pussy, pressing hard against the front wall as he spanks me again and again.

My mind is blank, my body like a stranger as Jack takes me so close to coming that I can taste the sweet pleasure on the tip of my tongue.

Then he stops.

The bed shifts, and his footsteps retreat across the room. I groan in disappointment, and he chuckles darkly.

"If you're a good girl…if you do everything I say, then maybe I'll let you come."

I press my thighs together, chasing the pleasure that's

receding fast. I know some women can come like this, but I'm not lucky enough to be one of them. What would Jack think if I could take what I need without his help? He'd probably be furious.

He returns with a knitted hat, which he puts over my head and eyes, blocking my vision. The material is too thick to see through and the light in the room is too dim. Without my sight, the panic inside me rises.

Jack's hands find the insides of my knees, and he pushes my legs open as wide as they will stretch. "You have a pretty pussy, Skye. So pink and soft." A rough finger drags wetness from my entrance up and over my clit, making me moan. Then his beard scratches the inside of my leg before his tongue laps at my pussy. Oh god, it feels different without all my senses. The control he has over my body pulls at my arousal like a piece of elastic stretched to its breaking point.

I moan and writhe at the exquisite pleasure, coming so close, I strain against the ropes on my wrists, but then he's gone.

Sound pours from me, tortured and desperate, and his laugh is wickedly pleased.

The bed shifts again, and a scraping sound from the corner of the room makes me flinch. Jack's returning footsteps are slow and ominous. "Are you ready?" he asks.

"For what?"

"I think you've earned your pleasure."

He opens a drawer to my right and flicks open a plastic lid. A squelching sound from a bottle cuts the silence. The sound of every one of Jack's movements is intense.

He uses rough fingers to spread my labia, and I gasp at the cool press of something big and blunt between my legs. It isn't Jack's cock. This is something different. He pushes whatever he has braced at my entrance harder. It's cool and slick but still burns as it enters me, and Jack groans with satisfaction at the graphic scene he's created. My consciousness seems to split from my body as the foreign object wedges deep inside me. His warm tongue laps at my clit as he moves the big implement back and forth, and I create an image in my head of what I must look like, spreadeagle and bound, in the total control of a wild mountain man whose twisted desires should feel terrible but threaten to split me open with pleasure.

"Oh god," I gasp.

"He can't help you here," Jack murmurs between my legs, pumping harder into me and flicking his tongue in short, vicious strokes.

What is he wielding? A dildo of some sort? A nightstick. My mind can't find one image to stick to.

He shoves it so hard, my toes curl and my back arches, and I cry out for him to do it harder, harder, harder. In the end, it's his relentlessness that shatters me, dragging me so deep into pleasure that I feel like I might never breathe again.

My body is a remote and shameful thing, twisting and spasming, grinding and moaning.

If I could look down upon myself, it would be with fascination and disgust.

"That's it, girl. That's it." The pleased tone of Jack's voice is foreign but welcome. He strokes my belly and thighs while I spasm through my orgasm, his gentle touch such a contrast to his overall attitude. When I'm finally still, he presses a kiss to my clit and reaches over my body, tearing the hat from my face.

Even though the room is dimly lit, my eyes still sting. Blinking fast, I take in the shape of Jack looming over me. I stare down the length of my body, desperate to know what's still wedged deep inside me. A long, thick wooden stick protrudes from between my legs, ending in a huge metal head.

Jack's ax. He fucked me with the handle of his ax.

Our eyes meet, and it's like looking into the face of the devil.

"Now you know what it's like to fuck a lumberjack," he

whispers, taking the ax and pulling it slowly from inside me. He holds it with the metal head downwards and brings the handle to his mouth, using his tongue to lick up my arousal.

My head drops back as my face heats with more shame. I tug at my wrist binds, but they're still holding strong. He rests his ax in the corner of the room and then climbs onto the bed. I press my legs together, but his hands are so strong that he forces them open without any effort at all. His cock is an angry bar that he wields like a weapon. Spreading his huge muscular body over mine, pinning me beneath his weight, we come face to face.

"Did you like it?"

I blink, frozen in his icy stare. If I say no, he'll laugh because he knows I did. If I say yes, I feel like I'm surrendering in a battle I never agreed to fight.

He eases his cock into my pussy so slowly, with our faces just an inch apart. He licks the underside of my top lip, smiling when I shift to accommodate his girth. "You like it dirty just as much as I do," he whispers, smiling again. Jack's teeth are so perfectly straight and white that they flash like a cartoon as the candle dances on the nightstand.

"No."

He thrusts hard, and my eyes roll back in my head. "Yes."

He thrusts again and twists his hips, rooting deep inside me.

"No."

"Yes." He bites my shoulder so hard, I yelp.

I'm a liar. Everything he does to me feels so good. My mouth is dry, but I still manage to whisper, "Please."

Then, from nowhere, I'm overtaken by another violent orgasm, and I lose control of my body. Jack holds me tightly while I jerk with the pleasure and fucks me as liquid streams warmly between my thighs. When he eventually comes inside me, he doesn't make a sound.

We are as close as two people can be, but the gulf between us is as vast as the Atlantic. Then he kisses my lips in the gentlest way, and I almost fracture with confusion.

Jack reaches out to untie my wrists, and he gathers me against his chest, so my body rests halfway over his. He takes my hand, brings my wrist to his lips, and presses a soft kiss to the bruised ring that encircles it. He kisses my forehead, moaning in a lazy, satisfied way.

I've given him what he needs, and now he's as content as a cat.

West was right. The key to keeping Jack happy is becoming a willing participant in his dark cravings. Just like I used to hate myself for pretending to enjoy Carter's pathetic attempts at sex, I hate myself for really enjoying Jack's twisted proclivities.

And if Jack can be like this, soft and compliant in the aftermath of sex, maybe he won't always need it to be so boundary-pushing.

"Do you want me to sleep here tonight?" I ask. The bed beneath me is damp, and even though Jack is a furnace, my skin erupts with goosebumps.

Jack stiffens, and his jaw hardens. It was the wrong thing to ask. Shit. Shit. Have I rejected him without intending to?

He pulls his arm from beneath my neck and urges me to sit. "Get out of here."

I stumble onto my shaky legs and reach for my clothes that cover the floor.

"Is that a c-section scar?" he asks abruptly.

"What?"

He draws a line across his abdomen with his hand. "Where's the baby?" My stomach lurches as he grins. "You gave it away? Typical deadbeat mom."

I choke on a sob, my heart splitting open at the horror of his words. I run from the room, shaking from my tears, trailing my hand over the walls until I find the door to my room in the darkness.

CHAPTER 8

SKYE

LOOKING BACK

It takes me more than an hour to calm down. At first, I huddled under the warm blanket, my body trembling at what happened. Jack's terrible words sliced open my already broken heart. *Deadbeat mom.* Is that what he thinks I am?

My body feels worn out and used, and between my legs, I'm sore but still vibrating with shame-filled arousal. Jack might be angry and spiteful, but he knows how to extract pleasure from my body in a way I can't even pretend to understand. I press my fingers to my lips, recalling how he kissed me gently. My wrists throb where he kissed them, too. In his arms, I felt totally safe until I didn't.

It was the same with Carter, I remind myself. He knew how to make me fall, and once I trusted him and let him into my heart, he started working to destroy me. I can't let

Jack do the same thing. I have to get better at shutting myself away. He can touch my body and use it for twisted reasons. He can extract all the violent pleasure from me that he wants, but I won't let him near my soul.

The power comes back on at some point and my room floods with light. I rise to put on my pajamas and find my phone. When I left Carter, I traded in my phone for a new one with a burner number so it couldn't be traced. My family disowned me, and my friends all fell away after Carter began to restrict my movements. There are no messages to check. No one in the world cares about me or knows where I am.

Instead, I flick through the news, wanting to feel connected to the outside world, even just a little. The local news site is filled with stories of corruption and violence, peppered with stupid feel-good stories like a picture of a cat who won a competition. I sigh, finding nothing to hold my attention until Carter's smiling face flicks up on my screen.

My breath catches in my lungs, my heart squeezing in one big thud that feels like it will be its last. 'Local businessman awarded new contract,' is the headline. I read through the article, finding out that Carter won a big contract to provide low-cost housing. He's been trying to get into construction for years, and I guess he's finally greased the right wheel. There's no way he has the expertise to run a company that builds housing. He'll throw them up in the cheapest way possible, and any inspectors will be bought off. It's how Carter always operates, leaving a sea of disaster in his wake. The poor people who will have to live in the resulting conditions are going to face unending problems.

But the figure quoted for the value of the contract is what sets the hairs rising on the back of my neck. A richer

Carter is a more dangerous Carter. It will give him even more power over Hallie, and indirectly over me.

The money I've made from this year-long contract won't be enough when I'm fighting against a man with politicians in his pockets. This is a disaster. Hopelessness swamps me.

I sob quietly into my hand, conscious that I could wake any of the three men in the rooms around mine. If I wake them, they might want sex, and I can't face more, even if they are rugged and good-looking, and they make it feel good when it shouldn't.

Hallie is out there somewhere, and not knowing where for sure is driving me crazy. I can't focus. I haven't eaten properly in weeks. The bones on my hips are now more prominent than they were when I first met Carter before Hallie made me plump.

Shona's face pops into my mind. We weren't friends. No one who worked for Carter would commit to anything other than passing communication with me. Even though I was often surrounded by people, he succeeded in isolating me. But I used to catch Shona looking at me with pity in her dark eyes. She would make me my favorite cocktail at the bar without me having to ask. Sometimes, she'd rest her hand on my arm if Carter was raging about something, and she'd witnessed me flinch. When Hallie was born, she gave her a sweet yellow rabbit and a rattle wrapped up in a pink tissue paper and ribbon bundle. Beneath was a box of chocolates for me, my favorites.

She wasn't my friend, but I felt a connection that she tried to conceal for fear of losing her job. She despised Carter, too. That was obvious in the way she'd stare at his back like she wished he'd drop down dead in front of her.

Is it enough to risk getting in touch and asking her about Hallie?

She might know nothing, but then again, she might know something crucial, and I don't think I can go on like this with worry flaring beneath my anxiety. I can't be a

72

deadbeat mom who isn't doing everything in my power to make sure my daughter is safe.

I pull up my messenger app and find Shona's number in my bag. I add her as a contact and type out a quick message.

Hey Shona, please don't share this number with anyone. I had to change it because of C. I'm far away in a place he'll never find me. I'm safe, but I don't have H with me. C took her. I don't know where she is, and it's driving me crazy with worry. I'm desperate. Have you seen her? Do you know where she is? Is she okay? I hope you're okay. If you can get out of there, you should. It's dangerous. He's dangerous. Do what I did and get away if you can. S

I don't put any names in the message, although leaving them out doesn't make it less obvious that it's from me. As soon as it's sent, my guts twist with worry. I don't think she'll tell Carter, but I can't know for sure. I think she's a good person, but knowing Carter has made me question my own sanity more times than I care to remember, and any trust I had in people withered away with my love for him.

I hope she'll tell me Hallie's okay.

My sweet princess will miss me. I know she will. The bond we formed is so strong that even a few weeks apart won't break it. *You'll be away for a year*, my mind whispers. *Even if you do get her back, she won't remember you after all that time.*

Whoever Carter has found to look after her will become her momma. His sister, maybe.

Tears drop from my eyes, staining my pajamas with dark spots before I can swipe them away. My empty breasts ache for my baby, making me curl in on myself.

I stare at the phone, waiting for Shona's reply, but nothing comes.

Have I made a mistake that will put my life in danger again? Have I risked the three lumberjacks who are my ticket to freedom once a year of contractual obligations is over?

You should read the contract, West urged me.

So, instead of focusing on a black screen or trying in vain to sleep, I find the contract and read it from beginning to end.

Shona doesn't reply.

So, now I'm not only worried about Hallie, I'm also worried that this cabin that's supposed to be my safe escape might become a place of danger from the outside as well as inside.

I close my eyes and try to conjure Hallie's sweet face.

I have to focus on each step it's going to take me to get her back.

I'm clear on everything Finn, West, and Jack expect of me.

Three-hundred-and sixty-three days to go, and then I'll find Hallie, even if it kills me.

CHAPTER 9

FINN

FORGIVE US OUR TRESPASSES

Early morning rain wakes me from a fitful night, the pounding on the cabin roof replacing the usual sound of chirping birds.

It matches the throbbing in my head.

My mouth is cardboard, and a lingering bitterness from the red wine is cloying in the back of my throat. I'm not a big drinker, and a wave of nausea ripples in my stomach.

How many of those damn shots did we do last night?

I slide out of bed and open my window, inhaling the fresh scent of damp earth, which suggests the rain has only just started. I hold out my hand, and I savor the cold, wet drops.

After living on the streets for so long, I appreciate everything about living in this cabin in this forest.

Jack's jibe last night hit me hard. He called me a stray dog. A fucking stray dog.

I know that he sometimes struggles to hold his tongue. He's gotten into many bar fights by unleashing that tongue on the wrong man. Jack's fierce enough and strong enough to come out on top most of the time, and he's always regretful after. He's a good man and has been more like family to me than I could expect of a stranger. But knowing all that doesn't make it hurt any less.

I spent much of the night tossing and turning. Jack was on a mission to rile us all, and he did a damn good job.

The season is changing now, and winter is coming. But this is the season that I love the most, exploring the forest, taking a pencil to sketch or some paints to capture the colors as they fade into paler shades. The frost begins to add a glistening effect to the landscape.

Skye seemed so happy last night, telling me and West about her love of painting and landscape. The memory brings me a small smile.

Today is Saturday, and the yard is closed until Monday, but there is still a lot to do.

I want to know what happened between Jack and Skye last night because something sure as hell did. West told her to go to him, something I wasn't happy about. But he was probably right.

Today is going to be the day that I invite Skye to see the studio. It's a work in progress, and I need West and Jack to help with some of the remaining physical tasks. It could be a way to encourage collaboration between everyone.

I crane my neck as a flash of blue catches my attention; it's Skye scuttling around the side of the house. She's wearing one of Jack's shirts and stooping against the rain. Moments later, she returns into view with some laundry, which she had hung out to dry, and she's moving speedily. I recognize some of my shirts and pants as well as a few of her much smaller items. She catches me watching and raises her hand, dropping some of her load onto the increasingly wet ground. I don't rush out to help her but instead notice how the damp air has lifted the bounce of her hair, framing her pretty face and how beneath the huge shirt that is swamping, she's wearing only a tank and her underwear.

The stirring in my boxers is immediate. Skye heads back into the cabin.

It's definitely time for a shower.

I don't close the window, leaving the crisp air to flood into the room to help clear the stuffiness that has built up overnight. And to let out my pent-up tension.

I'm not going to expect her to relieve me now.

Not when she's doing chores.

But later, it'll be my turn.

Dressed in loose pants and a fresh T-shirt, I stride into the hall and towards the kitchen. I don't need to tread carefully because Skye is already up. The men in this house can go fuck themselves.

She opens a cupboard as I approach and turns towards me, her nervous eyes roving first my face and then my body, taking me in.

I'm a big, powerful guy, and it feels good to have Skye's glances aimed in my direction. Even though it's a douche move, I tense my muscles in response and feel the tight fabric of my t-shirt stretch to accommodate the increased bulges of my biceps.

"Morning."

"Morning, Finn. I wanted to get the pancakes ready but had to get the clothes from the line! I'm really sorry!" Her eyes plead like she's worried I'm going to rage at her like Jack.

"Hey, relax! You don't need to explain yourself to me. I know you can't do two things at once, so no point trying!"

Her eyes are rimmed with red, and her cheeks are flushed pink, but her shoulders drop a little at my words. "Did you sleep well?"

I rub the back of my neck, still feeling the effects of yesterday's hard work. "Yeah. Okay. You?"

"I'm not used to the darkness and the silence. I think it's going to take some getting used to."

"If you ever need anything at night, just come find me."

She nods, and a smile flickers across her lips.

"Did things go okay with Jack last night?" The question is out of my mouth before I consider the repercussions. If she tells me no, what am I supposed to do about it? I'm allowing her to come between us by asking, doing exactly what Jack warned about. But I can't stand by if Jack's taking things too far. There have to be limits to what she can be expected to take.

"Yes. Fine." Her throat moves as she swallows what looks like a big ball of anxiety. She's keeping something to herself.

Is she used to brushing bad things away like nothing happened, pretending everything's okay?

Seeing her distress crushed me last night.

Skye turns her back to me, mixing the ingredients to make the pancake batter.

Who would blame her for wanting to leave?

I need to make sure she wants to stay.

Today, I'll show her that we have more to offer her than our testosterone-fueled bodies, dusty cabin, and foul tempers.

"I'll get some blueberries to go with that. We should have a box out front. It gets delivered every Saturday from Rango's store in town. It'll have most of what we need for the week ahead. We can add the things you want to it next week if you like. Or West or I can take you into town this afternoon. Anyway, I'll go see if it has arrived." She nods at me, and I head out to fetch our delivery.

To my surprise, both Jack and West are hauling firewood from the log pile where the tarpaulin keeping it dry seems to have slipped, leaving it exposed to the rain, which is now lashing down in great streaks.

"Hey, where are you guys gonna put that?" I step back onto the porch shelter, shielding myself from the rain.

"The barn." Jack says.

West stops what he's doing and glances my way, his face scrunched against the sheets of rain driving into him.

"Sleeping Beauty up yet?"

"Yeah, she's making us pancakes. Then we're all going back into the barn after breakfast to carry on setting up the studio. I need help with some of the carpentry."

Both men carry on dragging the wood into the barn, ignoring my comment, but at least they can think about my plan as I go inside to give Skye the box of groceries and show her where its contents live.

Inside, the sweet smell of the pancakes fills the entire kitchen. I drop the box next to Skye and take out packets, rummaging around for the berries. She has already set the table perfectly.

"Leave it to me, Finn. I'll get it all unpacked." Our eyes connect again; so much is unreadable in her expression.

She urges me to sit, and I feel a stirring of optimism. Through the window, I watch Jack and West tear off their waterproofs and sling them over the railing, discarding their boots at the porch door with a rumble that makes Skye startle.

They pull up seats at the table, and Skye approaches, balancing a huge plate piled high with steaming pancakes and presents it to us. I pray West doesn't ask for bacon or sausages, but thankfully he doesn't. We all immediately dig in, slathering the pancakes in syrup as she pours steaming cups of coffee.

Our bachelor pad is suddenly very homey and domesticated.

"So, what do you need to do over in the studio, Finn?"

Skye twists to listen to my answer to West's question.

"Lift and carry the materials and make some workbenches. Lacquer and varnish."

"Finn here considers himself an artist. He wants to turn the small barn into a 'studio.'" Jack uses his fingers to quote around the word studio, and Skye's eyes widen with surprise. It's the most he's said that hasn't involved him being pissed at someone.

"I started back in the spring, but we were sweating our bollocks off over the summer, so it all ground to a halt. I thought now would be a good time to get it all back on track so you can use it, too." I point at Skye with my fork.

She swallows a lump of pancake as if it is a rock stuck in her throat. She puts down her fork and blinks awkwardly. Is she about to cry? "Wh..." That is all she manages to say before standing abruptly and gathering the plates.

I don't offer to help this time because Jack is finally behaving normally, and I don't want to poke the angry bear.

Jack is focused on what's left of his pancakes, and West is gazing at Skye's bare legs like a hungry dog. There is no sign of her ass on show, but I'm pretty sure I know what he's thinking.

"Let's start at ten."

Jack shrugs, his lack of enthusiasm unsurprising, but he doesn't say no, so that's something.

The rain has stopped by the time we all reassemble, and the sun attempts to break through the clouds. I ask West to move the damp kindle wood into the storage area at the back of the barn to dry, and to collect the boxes of flat-pack units I ordered for workbenches and storage closets. As I open the box, slicing through the packaging and releasing the fresh smell of new materials, I sense Jack's urge to say something. His foot is tapping vigorously on the concrete floor, and he cuts in.

"I would have built you some units and benches."

"Yeah, I know, man. But you're busy at the yard. I didn't want to pile on any pressure. This is easier. I just need you to put it together properly. I've already started and not done the best job." I eye the half-built units and shrug. "They look like they've been assembled by a blind woodsman. Maybe West and Skye can lacquer?"

I look over at Skye, who has found my box of brushes and palettes. She cradles each item delicately between her fingers, mesmerized. She brings a brush to her nose and sniffs gently, closing her eyes and taking in its scent. She grazes the soft bristles of the brushes gently over her hands and cheeks, lost in thought. I wonder what memories she's recalling and whether they're happy or sad.

She's wearing tight-fitting jeans, which show off the curve of her thighs and ass, paired with a turtleneck sweater, clinging to her in all the right places. She's gonna get hot in here, and so are we with all that visual candy. West did well that first-night shopping for her.

"I want you to enjoy working here as much as I will," I say. "It'll keep you busy while we're at the yard." Looking up, Skye casts her questioning gaze between the three of us.

Her lips part, but she clamps them back together, turning away quickly.

Jack busies himself by lining up planks and screws, muttering obscenities under his breath, and West returns to lugging things about. I pass Skye the lacquer to apply to the units I finished in the spring. There is a purposeful atmosphere that feels like progress.

She accepts the brush and eyes the lacquer warily. "Can you show me?"

I demonstrate what I need her to do, and she observes and copies. I stay close, conscious that she's building her confidence around us. After five minutes, I'm about to leave when she says, "It's been a while since anyone did anything thoughtful for me...not since my parents, since..." Her voice trails off, and she lowers her gaze to the surface before her.

"This has been planned for a while. I just thought it would be something you'd enjoy, too."

She smiles shyly.

Conscious that we're making some group progress, I try to involve Jack. "Maybe Jack can show you how to carve wood."

"She's quite good with an ax, aren't you, Skye?" Jack cuts in and throws her a strange look that I can't work out. I want to say something, but Jack's face could freeze the sun.

Skye takes a deep breath. I notice the mottled red blotches appearing on her neck and chest. She's clearly overwhelmed.

"I'm going to the bathroom." Her words sound as if they come from far away, and she turns and flees from the studio, leaving nothing behind except the retreating sound of her ragged breathing echoing around the barn.

West downs his tool and approaches.

"Should I go after her?" I ask him.

A draft sweeps into the room from the now open door, swinging on its hinges. The weather has taken a turn, and the dark sky is angry and thick with threatening gray clouds. The rain is back, and the sound on the tin roof beats an urgent rhythm.

West shakes his head as if he doesn't understand what the hell is going on. I'm now sure that there is something that Skye is not telling us. She sold herself to us for a year, and we are still none the wiser as to why. And as much as I want her to stay and I'm enjoying having her around, I can't shake the discomfort I feel about it all.

This was supposed to be about creating some unity, some common ground.

Jack clears his throat and then speaks in a hushed tone, careful that his words are only audible to us. "Me and Skye, we were together last night." Jack's eyes drift to the door left open by Skye's hasty exit. "Not sure if either of you have noticed, but she has a scar. It's from a caesarian section birth. It's right there in the line of her panties. It's still pink, so it can't be that old. My guess is that she has had a baby sometime in the past year." He pauses and takes a breath, seeking acknowledgment from West and me to go on. "Yeah, well, you know what sort of state I was in last night. I wasn't choosing my words very carefully. When we were done, I asked her where her child was. And why did she think it was okay to abandon it somewhere because it clearly isn't here!"

Jack glances at the floor and tugs at this shirt collar, which he has buttoned right up to the top, tapping his right foot erratically. We remain silent for a moment. Words aren't always necessary to know what each other is thinking. But I can't help myself.

"For Christ's sake, Jack. Why'd you go make accusations like that? You don't know what happened."

Gritting his teeth, he lets out a ragged breath.

"I'm not proud, all right. But I damn well want to know what her deal is. And what sort of goddamn trouble she could bring to our door."

West has been quiet until now, but he says something that hasn't occurred to Jack or me. "What if she had a baby and it died?" I swallow hard on his words as they seem to echo around the studio with a life of their own, just as Skye reappears in the doorway.

If she heard what he said, she doesn't give anything away, returning to her abandoned task.

I meet West's gaze and Jack's, but no one says anything. West's suggestion would explain Skye's tears and her desperation to bury her past in the remoteness of the forest. Maybe the auction had nothing to do with money and had more to do with escape. Maybe she lied to me. Perhaps everything was too fresh and raw, and she couldn't deal with staying around where she'd be forced to remember every day.

And here is Jack, trying to force her to reveal her truth one way or another.

Secrets are kept for a reason, but they have a nasty habit of rearing up and injuring when revealed. Should we let her keep this one or make her tell us everything?

We while away a couple of hours before lunch and continue back in the studio in the afternoon. The mood seems to lift. Jack sings his entire repertoire of lumberjack songs. West joins in occasionally by slapping his hands against whichever wooden surface he's closest to. I tell Skye as many ridiculous stories as I can think of to ease her anxiety, like the time Jack tried to cook for Thanksgiving but forgot to thaw the turkey first or the time West fell face-first into the mud outside and freaked us out when he opened the door looking like a forest creature. And the time I knocked myself unconscious slipping in the shower three days after I moved into the cabin, forcing West and Jack to take me to the emergency room for a concussion. They had to dry and dress me before getting me in the car.

It feels good to laugh and collaborate on something where we can all bring our skills to the table. Skye seems to enjoy unpacking paints, pots, pencils, and a range of other materials. She goes back and forth between the barn and the cabin, bringing us drinks and snacks.

When Jack's throat is ragged, West sets up a speaker, and our project is lightened by the tones of Johnny Cash and The Backsliders.

By the end of the day, we've gone some way to make good progress on the studio project and show Skye that it doesn't have to be frosty between us.

The light outside begins to fade away, and the sounds of the rain and wind give way to the distant rustle of birds and other wildlife getting ready for the night shift.

As we're getting ready to leave, Skye clears her throat. "I know I had a difficult start, but I know what you expect of me now, and I want this to work, just like you all do." This time, her words aren't accompanied by tears or red blotches. She touches her neck, which feels like a nervous action, and I step forward to embrace her before Jack can spoil the moment with some other cryptic comment about axes.

Before I can cross the studio, the sound of footsteps outside, crunching against the undergrowth, roots us all to the spot.

A sense of unease takes over as Jack and West move quickly and quietly to the door. The look of sheer terror that sweeps across Skye's face tells us all that we need to know. *She's hiding from someone. She's on the run.*

But who from, and who's outside paying us an uninvited visit?

CHAPTER 10

WEST

SHADOWS OF THE PAST

Skye's body trembles, and her face is a frozen mask of fear. It's an extreme reaction to what is probably an animal rustling around in the undergrowth outside.

"Stay with Skye," I hiss at Finn. "Me and Jack will check outside."

Jack uses the bottom of his shirt to wipe the sweat and dust from his face. Outside, the forest is dark except for the small light over the front door of the cabin. My eyes sweep the area, finding nothing. Jack and I step out of the studio cautiously. Jack's holding a screwdriver at a vicious angle. I didn't think to come armed, but I have my fists, and they've served me fine over the years.

"Around the side." Jack angles his head and starts walking. For such a big, imposing man, he can move stealthily.

Jack's first to make it around the left side of the lodge,

and he comes to a stop. "Ethan, what the fuck are you doing?"

When I reach Jack, Ethan is pulling back from where he had his face pressed to the kitchen window. He straightens, then staggers a little, grinning with a mouth filled with stained teeth. The dude seriously needs to pay a visit to the dentist.

"Looking for the pretty girl you've got in there. I thought, if she's fucking three stinking lumberjacks, she wouldn't mind a fourth." He takes a step forward and teeters on his leg. I half expect him to fall to the floor in a heap, but he rights himself. "Where is she?"

Jack steps forward, holding the screwdriver facing down but clearly visible. He straightens so his shoulders expand, making his already huge form even broader. I join him, creating a barrier between Ethan and Skye, who's currently cowering in the studio. This fucking asshole isn't going to get anywhere near our girl.

"You need to get out of here." Jack's voice is calm, but there's an undercurrent of menace that could chill the Sahara. He doesn't talk about the things he's done in his life. As an ex-law enforcement officer, I can imagine there have been times he's stepped over the line. I know from my own military experience that in the heat of the moment, a lot can happen that seems terrible in the cold light of day. But Jack has a handle on the violence that lingers inside him like a specter. I do, too, but only to a certain point. Threaten me or threaten something that's mine, and it's over.

But you took something from him.

That's why he's here. Skye's just a cover. He wants to make me pay for Harold's death. Time doesn't change it. Going through the motions at work together won't change it, either. His brother died, and he blames me.

And I deserve the blame.

"I'm not going anywhere." Ethan lunges forward, his words slurring from a mouth that seems out of his control.

Jack holds his ground, and so do I. "This is our land, Ethan. And you're trespassing." Jack's weapon hand twitches, and Ethan's eyes drop to the long, sharp steel.

Even in his drunken state, it must register that he's in danger. Two against one isn't great odds when you're up against men who haul logs for a living.

"All I want is a taste. You owe me that much."

"I'll give you a taste of something," Jack says. "Your own fucking blood. Now, get out of here."

"YOU OWE ME..." Ethan's face contorts, reddening with fury as he points at me in jabbing motions. "YOU FUCKING OWE ME, WEST. YOU OWE ME A FUCKING BROTHER."

The torture in his voice tears at my heart. All the guilt I feel over being the one to escape the falling tree surges through my bloodstream. Harold's scared face as he shoved me out of the way and the way that expression didn't change when a huge branch caught him, crushing his body against the ground, is so clear in my mind.

I didn't deserve to live. He didn't deserve to die.

It was my mistake, and Harold paid with his life.

Now Ethan's suffering every day from grief.

"He doesn't owe you shit, Ethan. It was an accident. You know that. I know that. West knows that. Harold was a good guy, and he put his buddy's life before his own. He was a hero that day. And no pussy is going to bring him back. You aren't making any sense."

Jack takes a lumbering step forward, raising the screwdriver high enough to inspire panic in Ethan's eyes. One stab of its length would pierce his skull, and we'd be within our rights to deal with a trespasser on our land in the dark.

"All I want is a taste of that girl. What does it matter to you? You bought her. She's yours to pass around if you want."

"Fuck, Ethan. You're disgusting," Jack hisses. "Go find your own whore."

My head whips around to see if Skye's listening. Finn is at the open door of the studio, blocking her view of us, but voices carry in the silence of the looming trees on a now windless night. She's not a whore. I don't see her that way, anyway. Our contract agreement might involve sex, but that's only a part of what she's here for. I'd never look down on her for doing what she needs to do to survive.

Ethan staggers back, the alcohol destroying his coordination. His eyes are wide, and he mutters under his breath like a witch casting a spell. Something about how it should have been me that died that day, and how he curses my life.

He doesn't know how many times I wish it would have been me who died and Harold who'd lived. He was my friend, and the burden of his heroics has only crushed my life.

Skye's not a whore. She's a balm for three lonely, messed-up men who miss the company of a woman but are too fucked up to find one who'll stick around. She doesn't know it, but she has all the power.

"Just go," I tell Ethan. It's the strongest statement I can muster. "Just get out of here before we have to kick your ass."

"I HATE YOU," he spits. "I FUCKING HATE YOU."

"Yeah, well, we're not exactly in love with you either, man. Just go home and sober up."

Jack jerks forward, and Ethan stumbles backwards at the aggression.

"You could have just given her to me. I don't need her for long."

"GO!" I yell, not wanting to hear anymore.

"You can't watch her all the time, West." His eyes narrow at me as he takes another step back. "You have to work, and she'll be alone in this remote cabin." Ethan raises his hand to sweep across the lonely expanse of forest we're standing in. "I'll get her one way or another."

"I swear to god." Jack's restraint is gone in an instant, and so is mine. That's a direct threat to Skye, and he's not going to get away with it. Jack drops the screwdriver, realizing he won't need it against Ethan's drunk ass.

Jack's fist makes contact first, and Ethan is knocked to the ground. "You could have just left," he growls, laying another punch. I kick Ethan's leg, and he curls in on himself. "You could have left, but now you're putting me in a position where I have to teach you a fucking lesson."

Ethan's hands cover his face as Jack rains down another three blows. His flesh sinks around the toe of my work boot as I give him enough kicks to make him ever regret threatening to rape Skye.

"We should get rid of him," I say, tugging Jack's shoulder. He spins to face me, his eyes questioning. I didn't mean to kill him, but I can see just a flicker of the thought in Jack's eyes. "Throw him in the truck and dump his ass off in town."

"Good idea. Take his other arm."

Jack grabs Ethan beneath his left arm, and I take the right. He's a dead weight, and his head lolls in a weird, uncomfortable looking way. Jack didn't even hit him that hard, but the alcohol has him all fucked up. At the truck, Jack drops the back, and we shove him onto the flatbed on his back.

"I'll take him," Jack says. "Stay here with Finn and Skye."

I don't need him to clean up my mess, but I appreciate it. "Take the back roads. And dump him somewhere just outside town. Call Aiden or Caleb to pick him up. Explain what happened."

"No one is going to blame you, West." Jack slams the back of the truck, and Ethan groans. "They all know it could have happened to anyone. Ethan's becoming unreasonable."

Most lumberjacks are. If we were socially capable, we wouldn't choose to live in isolation.

"Just be careful," I tell him.

"Take Skye inside. Tell her enough that she won't worry. That girl has enough going on."

It's the first time I've heard Jack say anything remotely kind about Skye, but he's already stomping around the side of the truck and climbing in the driver's seat.

I watch as he disappears down the winding road from our property before I make my way back to the studio.

Finn's still waiting in the doorway, a shield between Skye and trouble.

"Let's get her inside."

He nods, and the way he looks at me, filled with pity, makes me want to scratch at my own skin.

Turning, he reaches for Skye's hand. She stares out into the darkness with wide eyes. "Ethan's gone, Skye. Jack's taking him far away. Let's go back to the lodge. She follows where Finn leads, her feet scuttling to keep up.

I follow close behind, unsure if my presence is reassuring or daunting.

Fuck. I can't stand to see her scared. Doesn't she realize we'll keep her safe, even if it costs us our lives? That's the kind of men we are. All of us.

I shut the door behind us and lock it, hoping the sound of metal on metal will make Skye feel more secure. Finn leads her to the couch and sits her down next to him. He throws his arm around her shoulder and pulls her against his chest, and she goes willingly, pressing her face into his dusty shirt.

I sit across from them in my favorite leather chair, letting my legs fall open, and my hands rest in my lap. My eyes meet Finn's, and he opens his eyes slightly, as though he's urging me to say something.

There are two things on my mind.

The things Ethan said and their impact on Skye, but also her terrified response to the sound of rustling before we even knew it was Ethan. Her reaction was extreme and way outside what I would expect from someone who wasn't running and hiding from someone or something.

"Ethan said some fucked up things, but he was drunk."

Skye's hand grips at Finn's shirt. She heard me but she's still scared.

"It's nothing to do with you, okay? He's angry with me, and he found a way to hit me where it hurts."

She turns her head slightly, her eyes focusing on mine, questioning.

"He knew coming here and talking about you would make me angry."

"Why?" she says.

"Because I don't accept anyone talking about someone…" I pause as I stumble over how to articulate what she is to me. Someone I own? That sounds fucked up, and she's more than that. Someone I care about? Care seems like a pathetic word, and Skye's only been here five minutes, but her sweetness and vulnerability have already found their way inside me, cracking resolve. "Someone I have a responsibility for," I finish.

She blinks, then stares at the floor.

"We've given him a warning. He won't be coming back."

"I'll be here alone."

"And he'll be at work."

Finn's expression shows his worry, but Skye doesn't see it. I have to ensure my own face remains impassive. "He's angry with me, Skye."

"Why?"

I don't want to tell her the reason. I don't want to open up that old wound for it to bleed out all over her, but I will so she'll understand. "Because I was responsible for his brother's death."

"It was an accident," Finn quickly interjects.

Skye's eyes never leave mine, and it feels like she's peeling up my skin and peering underneath for the truth at the heart of me. It's time to turn this around.

"I need to ask you something, Skye."

She stiffens slightly, and Finn's hand slides up her arm, keeping her close. "I saw your reaction to the possibility of someone being outside the studio. What are you running from? Because I know you're running from something."

"It's nothing," she whispers and then closes her eyes.

I could probe for more information. I could force Skye to confess, but what good would that do? As much as it frustrates me, we must work to earn her trust, and that will take time.

CHAPTER 11

JACK

INTO THE DARKNESS

I'm enveloped in darkness as the final traces of glowing embers fade, leaving nothing but a dying heat and lingering smoke. I inhale deeply and close my dry, gritty eyes. I'm so tired that my bones ache, and my head pounds in the rhythm of my heart.

The curse of insomnia has plagued my life for so damn long that I feel like the walking dead half the time. I surrender to the support of the chair I've tried to make myself comfortable in, one that I built with my own hands from the trees that I owe my life to. But there is nothing comfortable about sitting upright in the early hours of the morning. It is an agonizing torture, a punishment for all the wrongs I've committed.

Is it the deep-rooted loathing that grips me around the throat in a vice-like grip that prevents my mind from succumbing to a deep and refreshing sleep? The relentless memories of burning pain and shame, helplessness and disappointment? I flinch at the sudden recall of the power of a single set of approaching footsteps, of how I used to crouch in my closet and make myself as tiny as possible and close my eyes, hoping that my stepfather wouldn't see me.

Damn that goddamn son of a bitch.

My pulse quickens as I imagine how it would feel to beat him as he beat me, ruining his life like he did mine. One day, I'll find him and make him pay.

The constant pressure at the yard doesn't help. I've had to live with being wired and on high alert for more years than I care to remember.

When the rest of the house is quiet, and I'm alone with my thoughts, the darkness stretches on for endless hours. On a warm, dry night, I sometimes walk into the forest. As a boy, I used to run for the safety of the forest, hiding in the shadows and wishing I could build a treehouse high up in the safety of the tallest branches and live alongside nature and alone, not terrified to breathe in the house I was born in, with a mother who was supposed to protect me and a stepfather who wanted to destroy me.

But tonight, it's too cold, so I focus on the bright light of the moon shining a halo-like ring around the cluster of cedars in my line of sight. A light spattering of rain begins to tap against the window. My breathing slows and deepens, and my eyes feel heavy, waves of exhaustion pulling me down into the chair with an almost unbearable force...

A noise makes me jump. Was I asleep? I blink into the darkness. Damn, Ethan better not be creeping around out there again. I'll knock him from here to the river if he crosses this boundary one more time without my goddamn permission.

A soft creak of a floorboard and shuffling footsteps draw nearer. I can just about make out the trace of Skye's outline in the darkness. She's gliding like a ghost towards the porch door and choking on stifled sobs. With bare feet and dressed in a small pajama set, it's obvious she's not trying to escape.

I'm instantly on my feet to reach out to her.

Skye's soaked in sweat, her nightwear clinging to her like a second skin, and when she stops still, she sways slightly. She's still asleep and becomes distressed at my sudden movement, lashing out, thrashing, and flailing her arms around. Grabbing her again, I try to keep her restrained, but it only makes her worse. Her sobs become louder cries, and she tries to break from my grip.

"Skye, Skye! For fuck's sake, Skye!" I keep my voice hushed, not wanting to wake the others, and not wanting to alarm her further, but she is so lost in this night-terror or whatever it is that I don't know what else to do.

I try again, and this time, I lift her off her feet, cradling her like a baby, pressing her into my chest. She's a feather against my bulk, and a rush of protectiveness sweeps over me.

As I stride over to the chair, I remind myself that she's just an employee and nothing else. There's no room for any kind of feelings here other than ownership and lust.

I sink back down into the armchair, with Skye resting against my chest. Her warmth penetrates me through my threadbare shirt and boxer briefs. She's trembling, but no longer sobbing, and slowly, her eyes open.

"What happened? What's going on?" Her voice sounds like a frightened child, and she struggles again, like she wants to stand. I don't let her go.

"I think you were having some kind of nightmare," I tell her. "You were sleepwalking." Skye considers what I said, moving her gaze from the fire, and fixes me with beautiful eyes that I can only just make out.

"Can you light the fire, Jack? I'm so goddamn cold!"

She's talking like a lumberjack. Didn't take long. I can't help a half-smile.

"You were burning up back there." She shivers, and I

snort.

"Please, Jack."

I lift her with me as I rise and place her gently against the back of the armchair. Her hair is damp and sticks to the side of her face. She begins to shiver more in a way that makes me hurry my pace as I light the fire. It doesn't take long, and we both linger on the flame as it licks and rises into the cool air that has settled in the cabin. I'm pleased that Finn and West haven't woken, and I fix my gaze on the light of the moon, which is now casting its beam directly in through the cabin window. The clouds have given way to a clear, midnight sky. I inhale the first trace of heat as it rises from the hearth. Was I dreaming of the rain earlier?

In my periphery, Skye shivers again. There's a blanket over the back of the couch that I reach for as I make my way back to where she's sitting.

I don't expect her to lift her arms out to me, but she does with a needy, desperate look on her face. I scoop her up and sit back down, laying her across my lap. She rests her head against my chest as I pull the blanket around us both. She feels so small and so fragile. And helpless, too.

West and Finn suspect she's running from something. Maybe this is my opportunity to find out if they're right.

She lets out a small sigh, and for a moment, I think she has fallen asleep, but then her eyes open, and she stares at me.

"West told me he thinks you're on the run. Is it true?"

Skye ducks her head, lowering her gaze and pressing her face into my shirt. She trembles against me as though even thinking about what she's left behind is enough to fill her with fear.

In the doorway, the shadowy forms of Finn and West take shape, disturbed by Skye's cries, but I hold up my finger, stopping them in their tracks. They can listen but coming any further risks Skye clamming up.

My jaw tightens, and I tip her chin with my hand,

forcing her to look at me. "You're here with us now, and you need to know that we'll keep you safe, no matter what. But I don't like not knowing what kind of threat there might be waiting around the corner. You might be scared, and I get why some secrets are easier to keep, but you have to give us a fighting chance to face whatever might be coming so we can protect you."

A sob struggles form her throat, and she seems to shrink beneath the blanket. "He took my baby, Jack." Another sob rips from her, and I draw her closer.

"Who, Skye? Who took your baby."

"My husband, Carter Reynolds."

I know that name. He's a small-time gangster with big plans and blood on his hands. When I was in law enforcement, we had eyes on him for a small-scale drug operation, and his bar was thought to be a front for other nefarious activities. Lately, he's been in the papers for securing a big construction contract. He's dangerous because he has small-man syndrome, constantly trying to compensate for his self-hatred with grandiosity and bravado. Men like that are the worst kind to fall in love with.

I could tell Skye all this, but I don't want to layer anything else into her already overwhelming fear, so I remain silent but squeeze her a little tighter to signal for her to go on.

"She's only nine months old." Skye pauses, and her throat catches. She struggles to speak, and I can feel her adjusting her position in my lap. I hold her in a tighter hug.

"Leaving her behind has broken my heart. She's my world. My life. Carter took her, and he wouldn't give her back. I've no power against him. Not with all the terrible men he has on his payroll. I knew if I stayed and tried to find her, I'd end up dead somewhere. I had to keep myself alive. You have no idea what he's like." Her voice is now a whisper, as if it's easier for her to speak that way without crying. As if her words may not be real if she says them quietly enough. It's something I understand.

"He'll kill me if I go back, but the agony of staying away is tearing me apart every day."

She doesn't realize how much I understand her fear. Even when I left, I carried the fear so deep inside me that I thought I would never find a way to leave it behind.

Like a flame igniting, fury rises inside me, and I inhale a huge gulp of air but try to conceal my emotions.

"I haven't made many good choices in my life, Jack. I need the money from this to try to get Hallie back. I'm sorry...I didn't want to drag anyone else into this."

I kiss her forehead but hold the words that form quickly in my mind in the cage of my mouth. Nothing that comes quickly to me is ever productive. I need to think about what she's told me. And what is she planning on doing with the money exactly? A knot of unease twists in my gut.

I inhale deeply, my breath ragged in the silence of the room. The wind whips outside, and the cabin groans as though it's waiting impatiently for my response.

"Does he know where you are?" I ask eventually. It's key to understanding the risk to Skye and the danger that we'll all get drawn into a big problem with a wannabe gangster.

She shakes her head. "I didn't tell him what I was doing or where I was going. I left my phone behind." Skye exhales and then bites her lip, a sure sign she's holding onto something else.

"But..."

"He's been involved with the auction before. The man who runs it doesn't know I'm connected to Carter, but he'd remember me if shown a photo. The contracts have our names on them."

"And..." I say the word to make sure I've given her the opportunity to tell me everything.

"I sent a message to someone I think is a friend to find out if she knows anything about Hallie."

"Did she reply?"

Skye shakes her head, and her body shakes with sobs she's trying her best to suppress.

"So, she knows your new phone number?"

Skye blinks up at me, wide-eyed. "Yes."

"Can you trust her?"

The smallest shrug of Skye's shoulders tells me everything I need to know.

We sit in silence now, apart from the heavy sound of our breathing. I pull her in tighter and run my hand gently up the small of her back to her shoulder and down again.

She's no longer sweating, and she shivers slightly at my touch, especially when I make small circles against the thin cotton of her pajamas hanging loosely over her hip bones.

Her revelation doesn't surprise me. Her sheer terror tonight when Ethan appeared made it obvious that there was someone she was hiding from. Skye's put us all at risk, but I can't blame her. Having her baby taken from her has made her desperate, and desperate people do stupid, selfish things.

Carter might be a dangerous man, but we are all dangerous men when it comes to protecting what's ours. My jaw is granite. My hands flex into fists.

The guilt I feel about calling Skye a deadbeat mom forms a ball of shame that blocks my throat.

She's sold herself for the possibility of reclaiming her child. She's given everything she has for a small chance of saving her baby. This fragile woman is stronger than I ever could have imagined.

I think about my own mother and how much of my torture she witnessed and did nothing. She could have taken me and left. She could have tried to protect me, but she didn't.

My stepfather was a violent and vicious man, but my mom's apathy was worse.

Skye's hand bunches in my shirt, clutching at it like a baby gorilla grips its mother's fur. She turns her face into it, pressing a kiss against my heart. It's an act of sweet tenderness that jars. I haven't been a good man towards her. I've seen her as a threat to our way of life, but it's more than that. From the moment I saw her, I knew she had the power to get under my skin.

The air around us feels suddenly charged as she squirms in my lap.

"Jack." My name is a desperate, breathy plea.

I should resist what she's asking for. Crying women don't need sex. They need comfort and understanding.

At least women who've led happy and content lives need that.

People like Skye and me, who've experienced the worst of the world and been spat out on the other side, need different things altogether.

My cock thickening brings me back into the room. My hand glides like a silk thread to her waistline, and she gasps as my skin touches her soft, warm flesh. I trace my fingers over her ass and take one whole cheek in my open palm and squeeze gently, testing. She moans and adjusts herself, offering me her sweet spots, pushing herself back against my open hand. I linger for a moment and allow my hand to squeeze again before trailing my fingers down around the outside of her exposed ass.

Stroking over and over her covered pussy, the heat of her increases with every pass. She swivels herself around to face me directly and drops her knees wide open.

My cock is throbbing for release, and the night is still stretched out before us.

I stand and lay her down on the rug in front of the fire, dropping my boxers to the floor and stepping out of them in a fluid movement. She watches me the whole time and moans at the sight of my huge length, which aches with violent need. Blood rushes to my head as I fist it tightly, watching as she removes her nightwear.

"Rub yourself, Skye. Finger your pussy but don't come. Get yourself ready for me," I growl, but I'm hungry, not angry.

She watches me as I give myself a couple of quick jerks to show her how ready I am. I move swiftly for someone so lumbering and rummage around in the cabinet next to the fire until I find what I want. We don't have much call for curtain tiebacks, so these have been stored in the drawer for the better part of a decade.

As I approach Skye, she sits with her legs wide open and offers her wrists out to me with uncertainty. She knows what I like. She knows how good it can feel. I hope she knows I wouldn't hurt her outside of where it feels good.

"Make it hurt," she whispers.

She closes her eyes and inhales slowly. Her body trembles, but I'm unsure whether it's the warmth of the flames beginning to work their magic or the anticipation of what I'm about to do to her.

Or is it fear?

She's lost in herself and looks like she's meditating, preparing herself for what's coming next. *Punishment or reward,* depending on how you look at it.

Looking towards the doorway to the hall, I signal for Finn and West to come forward. They've been silent and observing, and I know that they heard everything.

Casting my gaze back to Skye, who's waiting with her arms outstretched, still presenting her wrists to me, I step forward, drop to my knees, and bind them together.

She needs this, and I understand why.

I can release her from the shackles of her tortured heart and soul.

I can do that much for her.

I signal them both to approach further as Skye slowly opens her eyes.

CHAPTER 12

SKYE

HIDING FROM THE TRUTH

Jack knows my truth. There's no hiding anything from him anymore. He knows, and he cradled me while I cried and kissed me so sweetly my heart ached. He showed me the sympathy I never expected.

And now he's found a way to give me what I need to step out of my turmoil for a while.

Guilt prickles beneath my skin for wanting to get lost in pleasure and pain when Hallie should be the center of all my focus, but missing her is destroying me, piece by piece. I have to find a way to preserve what little is left to fight for her.

The sound of feet on the hardwood forces me to twist. Almost entirely concealed by shadows, Finn and West enter from the hallway. How long have they been there? Did they hear my confession? Did they see me break and Jack attempt to put me back together?

Finn drops to his knees, bending so his face is close to mine. "Skye, is this what you want?"

He touches a tear that's leaked from the corner of my eye.

"Yes." I blink, and another tear comes loose. His eyes follow its path into my hair and are filled with so much concern it makes me want to weep more.

"Just forget about the contract tonight," West says firmly. "We don't have any expectations of you while you're upset."

My mouth drops open with surprise. I'm naked and bound on the living room rug, and he's hard as a rock beneath his gray sleep shorts. But he's prepared to let me get dressed and go to my room alone if that's what I want.

I let my gaze pass over them all, realizing suddenly that they're all different men than I thought. Or maybe different is the wrong word. The way they dressed my room before I arrived, protected me from Ethan, and gave me pleasure; all those things displayed their character. They were just overwhelmed by the darker aspects of restriction and Jack's temper, which has now dropped away like a skin he's outgrown.

Their kindness and care only make me want this more.

"I need this." My voice is so raspy, but it has an urgency that they seem to understand. Finn looks first to West and then to Jack, and whatever passes between them leads to Finn kissing my lips with a gentle softness that wraps warmly around my heart. West drops to his knees, too, trailing his warm, calloused palm over my belly and breasts. The rough parts, developed by swinging an ax or wielding a chainsaw, make me shiver with every pass.

Finn kisses down my throat, making soft, appreciative sounds as I close my eyes.

Jack bends between my legs and kisses the inside of my thigh. It's a sweet gesture, but then he bites hard enough to make me jump, and I expel a long breath of relief. He kisses the spot he hurt, and I let my legs drop further open, inviting him to do more.

My craving for pain still confuses me. The peace I find in it is strange and intoxicating.

When he repeats the mix of kisses and bites on the other side, I groan loudly.

"She likes that," West says. His fingers move from caressing gently to pinching my nipple hard enough to make me yelp. When he wraps his hot mouth around it to soothe, my hips arch, searching for contact.

"We've got you, Skye," Finn says, and I stare up at him with wide eyes, sensing that he's talking so much more broadly than about this physical act at this moment.

"Lick her," West tells Jack. "Get her off. Then we can fuck her." He stares down at me with butter-soft eyes and strokes his capable hand down my face. "That's what you need, isn't it, baby?"

"Yes." It's an admission that floods my face with hot shame and my pussy with greedy heat.

Jack's tongue is like a weapon, rasping over my soft flesh with a determination that feels too much. He probes my entrance with two and then three thick fingers, and my toes curl against the soft rug, craving the twist of his knuckles like crack.

With my hands bound, I can't reach for Finn or West in the way I'd like, but I still have my mouth.

"Show me." I twist my head and gesture to Finn's cock.

He shoves off his striped shorts in a flash, revealing his very big, very hard cock. His hair flops over his forehead as he strokes it in his huge palm. I slick my tongue over my lower lip, ready.

All the chaos in my mind slips away as he shifts closer to stroke the tip across my mouth. Staring up at Finn's looming form makes me woozy. Stacked muscles carve out his belly, leading up to rounded pecs, thick biceps, and corded forearms. His expression is lost, as though the prospect of sliding into my mouth is too arousing for him to handle. I open wide, craving to be filled.

And Finn doesn't disappoint.

The angle is awkward, and I have to hold my jaw open so wide to accommodate him that it aches, but the pain takes away from the ache in my heart, and when West presses my wrists against the floor, exerting more control, my grip on reality slips away.

I'm close. So close that my thighs tremble. So close that when West tweaks my nipple again and Jack's tongue flicks just right, I'm swamped in a pulse of dark pleasure that threatens to drag me under so deeply, that I feel like I'm never going to claw my way back.

Finn draws back as I groan loudly, trembling and shaking, but Jack's hand holds me steady, spanning my whole belly, and West's does the same as he rests it over my heart.

"She's ready," Jack says, speaking about me like I'm not in the room. In a way, it feels true. The disconnection of my mind and my body has been solidified by the twisting bite of pain and flush of pleasure.

He does something I don't expect and stands, gazing down at me with eyes that burn and a chest that rises and falls like he's just finished sprinting through the forest. He was in the right place to go first, but instead, he gestures to West to take his place. It's a selfless move that I wouldn't have thought would fit with Jack, but the more I get to know him, the more I see who he truly is.

A man who cares deeply about his friends.

A man who would step in to protect the people he loves and even a woman he barely knows.

A man with a moral code which conflicts with his dark and twisted sexual fantasies and his need to control.

A man with emotional burdens and torment of his own.

West runs his fingers through the soft curls between my legs and uses his thumbs to spread me open so he can taste me. He savors me for three swipes of his tongue, inhaling deeply, then he shifts until his big, thick cock is pressed to my entrance. "Ready?"

"Yes."

With a hand on my waist and his powerful thighs pressed to the underside of mine, he pushes deep, and my body takes him in with no resistance. I watch him fuck into me, in awe at the controlled motion of his hips and the flexing of his abs with every thrust. His chest is so big and broad, and his arms muscular and powerful, capable of so much destruction. The dusting of hair across his chest and his dark beard give him a dark masculinity that I didn't know I'd like, but find I crave.

Jack twists my face, kissing me with a mouth that still tastes of my pleasure. His hand grips my throat, holding just a bit tighter than he needs to, making my head swim.

But I don't feel unsafe.

I feel surrounded. These men are like a cocoon against the world.

Strong and fierce, they worship my naked body like it's an altar to Mother Nature who gives them shelter and a way to earn a living.

And I take it. I take it all.

I clutch at West's hips with my legs, drawing him deeper, urging him to go faster and harder. Gripping my waist, he pulls me into each thrust until I ache with the depth of his penetration.

Finn's finger presses just above my clit, and a look passes between the two men, one of collaboration. Jack teases my nipples, wetting his finger and circling, leaving a cold trail of sensation that connects directly to my pussy, and I can't stop the barreling pleasure that knocks my mind into an abyss of pleasure.

"Oh god, oh god, oh god," I cry out.

"That's it," Jack says, his voice curled with a smile. "Fuck, that must hit nice."

West groans, his cock swelling then pulsing as he empties all his power inside me, still moving through both our orgasms.

He falls back onto his heels, panting like he ran up a hill, bracing his huge hands on the floor next to him. Between his legs, his still semi-hard cock is glistening, and the thatch of hair around it is messy with both our arousal. I want to reach out and touch him, but I can't, and my fingers flex within my binds.

"Finn?" West asks.

Finn gestures to Jack to go next, always the man with the biggest and least selfish heart, and I'm surprised to see Jack initially saying no. Eventually, when I moan for more, desperate for even greater obliteration, West moves out of the way, and Jack flips me onto my front. My breasts press into the warm rug, and I have to twist my face away, staring at my left arm, which is still anchored over my head. Course hands slide up my thighs and over my ass, softly at first but then with more pressure.

"She has such a pretty ass," Jack muses.

"She has a pretty everything," Finn agrees.

"Prettiest pussy I ever saw." West moves my hair from around my neck and brings his mouth close to my ear. "I can still taste it," he whispers, then licks at the same time that Jack lifts me onto my knees. A single finger slicks over my engorged clit, and the pleasure-pain makes me cry out.

Before I have a chance to anticipate anything more, he shoves his cock deep. I'm messily wet, so the slide is easy, but he's thick and long and demanding as his balls slap against my pussy. "This is what we need, Skye," he says. "This is what you need, isn't it? Raw, filthy fucking that makes you feel alive."

I flush so hot that sweat beads on my upper lip and around my hairline. It's impossible for me to feel alive without my baby. I'm a dead woman masquerading—a naked mannequin in a derelict shop.

Digging his fingers into my ass, he spreads me wide and presses into my taint until his thumb is up to the knuckle and moving with every thrust of his hips. "Oh…oh…oh," I gasp, as some unholy connection begins to draw together a tsunami of pleasure.

"You like my thumb in your ass?"

"Yes." It's a gasp that leaves my lips without proper consideration. I shouldn't like it. It's not something I've ever considered, but now he knows the truth, he'll want to push further. That's what Jack is like. He takes and takes, even when I'm not sure I want to give.

He proves me wrong every time.

"Holy fuck," Finn groans as he touches my face, and I take his finger into my mouth, sucking hard.

"She wants every hole filled," Jack says. "Hold her."

He must indicate something to West behind my back because suddenly West supports my upper body so I can rest on my bound wrists without hurting myself. "Put your cock in her mouth." West's instruction is said darkly, huskily, like he can't wait to see what that will look like.

Finn seems uncertain but only until I take him so deeply, I gag. He tastes salty-sweet and swells as I swirl my tongue around his swollen head. He touches my cheek so sweetly as though he wants to soothe my overstretched jaw.

I wonder what I must look like, held by one man while another fucks my face and another fucks my pussy and penetrates my ass. A body used to within an inch of its capacity.

The girl I used to be, sweet and innocent and dreaming of love, is gone, and in her place is someone ragged and torn and desperate.

Pleasure surges in a way I've never experienced before. My body won't stay still, trembling and shuddering as all my nerve endings flash bright. Finn's cock slips from my mouth, and Jack comes with a growl, pounding into me like he's forgotten I'm a person. My pussy is just a vessel for his pleasure.

I must black out because, for the longest time, there is nothing.

I'm wiped clean. No past. No present. No future.

Bones and flesh. Pleasure and pain. And nothing in between.

CHAPTER 13

FINN

A BAND OF BROTHERS

In the glow of the fire, my eyes trace the lines of Skye's body as she slowly and rhythmically grinds herself into Jack's pelvis. His eyes are clamped shut so she swivels her gaze to connect slowly, first with West and then with me.

Her tiny, lean body is like a doll against his solid, muscular powerhouse. How a woman's body can so easily welcome the bulk and force of a man's desires as he drives deep inside her has always fascinated me. How does she not break?

She momentarily closes her eyes and moans under her breath as he withdraws.

I shift to distract myself from the throbbing between my thighs. I still feel the sensation of her mouth around my cock, and all I want now is to bury myself inside her. I realize that I have let out a moan of my own and catch myself, suddenly self-aware, self-conscious. West is opposite me, but I don't look at him. He adjusts himself, already recovered from his time with Skye.

"Finn." She holds my gaze, and I'm momentarily transfixed by her stare but my heart is hammering and adrenaline is coursing through my body like electricity. Every part of me wants to touch her and to feel the mental and physical connection. My mind concedes, and I take the place Jack has vacated.

Between Skye's legs is a mess of my friend's arousal. Fuck. She's already taken so much, and I'm not like my buddies. I want to counterbalance Jack's strength and West's intensity. I want to give her a soft landing. I emit another low moan, and another rush of blood surges to my cock. I don't think I've ever been so hard or so afraid of the tension that has hijacked my body.

"Touch me!" She whispers so quietly, so gently, and yet the fire in her eyes is fierce.

I place my left hand on her right breast, and I stroke and squeeze.

"Does that feel good?"

She nods, biting her lip.

It's my turn now.

I trail my hand down her body with one hand, and with the other, I circle the head of my cock around her clit, letting out a huge sigh. In one long, hard, and deep thrust, I'm inside her. I grind into her, losing myself in the physical reactions of my body. Skye pants softly, and as I brace myself over her, her breath is hot and gentle against my neck.

"Finn." The whisper of her voice is a plea.

Slowing my rhythm and catching my breath, I luxuriate in the moment with slow, languid movements that feel so damned good. Skye lifts her knees up around my waist and pushes her hips forward. I'm deeper inside her, and she's clenching around me, her muscles gripping with greater force. I won't be able to last much longer.

All I can think of is how good she feels and how much

I want to give her.

She's lost a child.

She's come to us for safety and the chance to reclaim her baby.

This pleasure is easy to give her. The sweet release is simple. But rebuilding her life once our contract is done won't be so easy.

Maybe we can help.

I burrow my face into Skye's neck, and as she spasms around me, I release inside her.

Skye isn't just a woman who sold her body for a year. She's a beautiful person with a mission that breaks my heart.

I wrap my arms around her and hold her tightly against me. Realizing her hands are still bound, I loosen them so she can embrace me, and the feel of her arms wrapped around me is bliss. She's so tiny, but there's a fierceness in her grip that conveys so much.

Tonight, we've all achieved a greater understanding and connection.

But we're going to have to decide what to do next.

Skye needs us.

I know what it's like to lose people; first, my mom to a sudden illness, then my sister to adoption. I was older and left in foster care until the home became dangerous, and I decided I'd be safer on my own.

Jack and West know the pain of loss in their own ways. West carries guilt over Harold but also unspoken horrors from his service. Jack's home life was terrible. It's part of why he finds it so hard to trust women and the fuel behind his rage.

We tread carefully around each other when we need to. We tolerate each other's crap, and all is forgiven when it goes wrong.

But like brothers, there is an urge to protect, to look out for each other, and to keep our business between these four walls despite the things that cause friction.

Skye coming into our lives has given us a shared purpose. She's ours to protect. Ours to care for. This cabin, this forest; this is home.

What will it take to heal our wounds and right all the wrongs?

Maybe more than any of us can achieve.

But we can try.

For Skye, we can try.

CHAPTER 14

JACK

A SEED OF A PLAN

As Skye rests in Finn's arms, I'm suddenly taken aback by a wave of protectiveness towards this woman who has come into our lives. The moment I saw her, I had a feeling in my gut. I thought that feeling meant trouble, and maybe it still does, or maybe it was a sense that she was destined to become something bigger in our lives.

I know West and Finn feel the same way.

It's as if we've been given this woman who needs our help, and now we have to look outside of our own lives and rise up like her knights in shining armor.

I remember the night I saw Finn huddled on the sidewalk outside Rangos. I could have walked past him, but something told me to talk to him. The rest is history. Sitting here tonight, I have the same urge to help Skye, and as much as I try to push the sensation away and lock it up with a heavy-duty padlock, I can't deny the anger that has gripped me hearing what that man has done to her.

The heat from the fire I hastily stoked is dying, and the light in the room is fading along with it. It won't be long until the sun begins its ascent. Skye looks exhausted as she disentangles herself from Finn and moves onto the couch. He rises, too, stretching his arms above his head as he follows Skye and wraps her in a blanket. West guzzles water as if it's the height of summer and he's decimated half the forest with his ax.

"Thirsty work. I thought Skye was here to ease the strain, not make us bust a gut!" We both stifle laughter, even though no one's sleeping yet.

"We're getting old," I joke.

"Speak for yourself. I'm in the prime of my fucking life." West rubs his abs, unconscious of the jut of his cock, proving his sentiment right now. The man's ready to go again, although it's doubtful Skye could face more of our brand of sex right now.

I pull on my shorts and toss West his. He tugs them up his thick legs, adjusting his cock so the waistband holds it in place.

We both sit at the table, even though it's the middle of the night, and we all need to sleep. I lean in, keeping my voice low so Skye won't hear.

"It's fucked up what she said, though, right?"

"Yep."

I know that this will be something West wants to put right. He has too many stories from his days in the military, where justice and retribution were distant or impossible. Our simmering frustrations could be put to good use.

"We're gonna need to do something about it."

"Yep."

Our eyes meet and silent confirmation passes between us. Whatever it takes is what we both communicate.

"I'm gonna put Sleeping Beauty to bed. Sunday tomorrow."

116

West nods, guzzles another slug of water, and returns the glass to the sink.

As I stoop down to scoop Skye from the safety and comfort of Finn's lap on the couch, I catch her sweet and now almost familiar scent and lift her with ease. She's like a feather in my arms, already half asleep, and she stirs a little before wrapping her arms around my neck. Her pale skin is warm against my rough and calloused hands. I tread carefully into the hallway and along to her room.

From her window, the lingering glow of the moon is fading and I can already hear the first of the early morning birds begin their dawn chorus. What time is it? She doesn't have a clock, and I can't see any sign of the burner phone.

I reach out to draw back her cover and lay her gently on the bed below. I grab the blanket that West left for her, hanging idly over the back of my rocking chair, and spread it over her slim frame.

Her body is curled in on itself in a protective pose. I watch her as she stirs and settles, and my eyes wander over to the window. The curtains are undrawn, and the space behind the glass is as black as Satan's heart.

Casting my gaze back down, I'm caught off guard to see Skye's eyes wide open. She reaches out for my hand, which I accept.

"I didn't abandon her, Jack. I would never, could never. I can barely breathe without her. I'm glad I told you."

I sit with her words. Shivering with the cold settling around the cabin, I inhale deeply, closing my eyes.

"And when we do what we do together, it doesn't mean I've switched off because I don't care. But … it just helps me to almost express the pain that I feel. I can channel my energy, my helplessness, my frustration, if that makes sense."

It makes perfect sense. Connecting to disconnect.

A crushing image of my mum standing helplessly in my bedroom doorway while my stepfather dragged me out of my closet by my hair and stamped on me with his goddamn boots flashes into my mind. He struggled to remove his belt from his pants before beating ten tons of shit out of me. Disconnecting was the only way to get through it because crying never did a goddamned thing. Mom never tried to stop him. The look on her face was calm, cold, indifferent.

I flinch at the recall, and Skye sits up in response. She doesn't say anything, but her presence is a comfort I couldn't have predicted.

"I'm not proud of what I said to you." It's the closest thing to an apology that I can manage.

Skye nods, clutching the blanket high around her neck.

"I know what it's like to live in fear, Skye. My mother. She wasn't like you. She stood by and let my stepfather beat me."

"Jack…" Her expression is as broken as I feel.

"She's got what she deserves. She's rotting in a care home somewhere. I hope her guilt is eating her from the inside out."

"And what about your stepfather?"

I shrug. I don't know where he is because if I did, I'd put him six feet under with no remorse.

"You are not on your own, Skye. Not anymore."

I lay her back down under the cover and tuck the blanket around her. She closes her eyes, her lids flickering gently. My body shivers as I stroke her soft hair.

Although the morning is approaching already, I'm going to throw on something warm, get under the covers of my bed, and try to get the sleep I so desperately need. Silently, I leave the room, closing the door and turning towards my end of the hallway. Skye is breathing steadily before I even leave the room.

Once I'm in the familiar four walls of my space, I light a lamp and pick up the clean cotton boxers and my favorite fleece shirt that Skye placed in a laundry pile. She folded everything with military precision. West will be pleased.

I wonder if her ex, Carter, forced her to be like this.

Asshole.

Skye isn't like any woman I've met before. She's prepared to sell herself to three strangers for a whole year to save her only daughter. Hallie is one lucky little girl to have a mother who loves her so much.

I lay myself down wearily, stretching out to fill my bed. My heavy eyelids flicker, my body sinks slowly into the mattress, and my overactive mind is forced into shutdown.

But as I pray for sleep to take me over, I find myself grappling with an emerging thought, rising from the darkest crevices of my mind.

Bill Tappin. *You owe me.*

I wake too early, exhaustion still weighing heavy. The sun is up, but the clock reads the ass crack of dawn. I wish I could sleep for longer, but I know from experience that trying only ends in frustration.

Surprising myself, I'm almost considerate as I emerge into the corridor and pad softly along the floorboards and into the kitchen. I don't want to wake anyone. It was a tough night.

I shake my head. I'm turning fucking soft.

I'm surprised to see both Finn and West already at the table, huddled and talking in whispers.

"Couldn't sleep either?" I roll my eyes. They know me and sleep aren't the best of friends, but West's comment suits the mood.

"Fix me a coffee, someone!"

"Course, man."

I watch Finn as he lumbers over to the machine. He returns, places a steaming hot mug in front of me, and I lower my head to inhale the rich scented steam. I need this caffeine hit to yank me into the land of the living.

"I guess Skye is still out for the count."

"Yup, I checked a few moments ago, and she's dead to the world!" Funny, I didn't hear him; I guess he was fairy-footed, too.

West slides his phone across the table as I take my first bitter sip. The face of Carter Reynolds, Skye's ex, looks back at me from the screen. The man's a weasel, smugness radiating off the newspaper's front page, a coldness discernable in his cesspit eyes. Anger bubbles against the back of my throat, making me grit my teeth. I glance between Finn and West, trying to read their thoughts.

"Is this the dude Skye is married to? West couldn't shake the name once she had said it, and when we saw this, we realized."

I give Finn a grim nod. "Yep. That scum bag is rotten to his core."

"Are we at risk, Jack?" Finn's expression is concerned, but West looks like he's preparing for battle, veins bulging in his neck and the tattoos on his bare arms depicting signs of a soul ready to torture for what he wants.

"Put it this way, some of his men make us look like saints. But I reckon that if pushed, they'd regret ever laying eyes on us!"

"So, what are we gonna do about it? What are you saying?" Finn's eyes are questioning.

Finding Carter Reynolds and helping Skye reunite with her daughter, Hallie, is something we need to consider.

West rubs the back of his neck. "So we're gonna get this motherfucker then, Jack?" He says it like it is.

Carter Reynolds poses a threat to us all. To Skye for having the courage to break away and possibly take what he thinks is his, and us, for standing by her side.

He's a direct threat to someone who belongs to us now.

And he's holding in his possession someone else that we want: Hallie.

"That's exactly what I'm saying, West. And this is how

it's going to happen…"

We spend the next hour reviewing our ideas, each of us pointing out pitfalls and risks. Between us, we bring all that is needed: strategy, tactical solutions, brute strength, a willingness to succeed, and a drive to protect what is ours.

And by the time Skye has surfaced from whatever kind of rest she found, we've shaped the beginnings of a plan.

Carter, son-of-a-bitch Reynolds, will regret the day he was born.

I'm going to make sure of that, personally.

CHAPTER 15

WEST

UNDER THE COVER OF DARKNESS

The bar that Carter Reynolds operates his bottom-feeding criminal empire from is a dive. In our truck, Finn observes the door through a pair of binoculars. I keep a watch on people coming and going, taking the occasional photo. My right arm is stiff from work. Mondays are usually the worst, like my muscles adapt to rest over the weekend and object when they're asked to labor again.

Jack's idea was to stake out the place for a night to gauge the kind of threat we might be dealing with. I take pictures and send them to Jack to see if he can identify anyone. We're yet to see Carter himself, but the night is young.

Jack stayed at the lodge with Skye because there's a chance he'll get recognized from his days as a cop. Criminals have long memories, and none of us want Carter spooked before we can deal with him and get Hallie back.

"This place is a cesspit," Finn says. "Look at this goon."

A colossal man lumbers from the door, his belly so broad, he can barely fit through the doorway. His head seems so tiny compared to his body, like a grape resting on a melon. He shuffles, pulling his phone from his pocket and bringing it to his ear. Not for the first time, I consider law enforcement to be an interesting career, at least some of the time. I couldn't do it, though. I've become addicted to the forest and working with my hands. If my body isn't sore by the end of the day, I feel like I haven't done enough. The donuts could be cool, though.

"I can't imagine Skye in this world."

Finn nods in agreement, leaning closer to the window as a woman exits behind the goon. "She's too gentle," he says. "Too sweet for this life."

The woman is wearing a leather skirt, high-heeled ankle boots, and a tube top that barely holds anything in place. She struts like she's walking the hooker catwalk. "That woman belongs here." I tut as she drapes herself over a man who just got out of a huge black SUV. He shoves his hand up her skirt and palms her tit in full view of everyone.

"Maybe," Finn says, lowering the binoculars and facing me. "Or maybe she's been forced into this life and is playing along so she doesn't get hurt. Isn't that what Skye must have done before she left."

The idea of Skye acting for self-preservation is like a knife to the gut, especially if she had to sell her body.

You bought her body, I remind myself.

But it's different. We never wanted to hurt Skye. It was always a simple money-for-service exchange. And we always intended to provide her with somewhere safe to live and maybe more if she wanted it. Somewhere she wouldn't mind being, even if she did have to work.

We're not the kind of men to ever use a woman without giving her pleasure, too. That has to count for something.

"There's no way we're going to see the baby here," Finn says, refocusing on the door.

"Why? Because it's late?"

"Yeah. Why would anyone in their right mind bring a baby to this hole?"

"Carter's not exactly winning father-of-the-year, though, is he?"

"We should go inside."

I tip my head from side to side, releasing tension as the woman in leather is practically carried inside by the man with greedy hands. Do I want to go into that dive? Definitely not. This kind of place makes me feel uncomfortable to my bones, but will I do it for Skye? Absolutely.

As we slide out of the truck, I'm struck by how out of place I feel. Reggie's bar isn't like this. It's for working men to let off steam, not for criminals to network. Men like this are on the edge, ready to fly off the handle for virtually no reason. They take one look at a person and immediately decide if they like them or not.

Me and Finn can handle ourselves but I don't want to have to. Mostly, I don't want to draw attention to us now in case it risks our future involvement in this situation.

"We need to keep a low profile."

Finn nods, sliding his hands into his pockets. He's wearing a plain blue shirt, and a dark blue baseball cap to shadow his features. I opted for a black sweater and a beanie, which I've pulled low over my forehead. My dark beard almost obliterates the rest of my face.

There are two security guards on the door which is unusual for a bar. They give us the once-over, maybe because they haven't seen us before, and this place is mostly visited by regulars. "You're not going to give us any trouble, are you?" One of them addresses me, slightly shifting to block me from entering.

"We're just here to have a drink. Maybe find some

pussy," I say, hoping that will be enough to satisfy him. It is, and he moves aside.

"Be careful with the pussy." He screws his nose up as though he's smelling something filthy. "A lot of the girls in here have been passed around more times than I can count."

"Easy pussy's good as long as it's clean," I say with a shrug.

He laughs and nods at us as we pass. "Have a good night."

When we're inside, the music hits like a wave. It's some kind of grunge rock with so much strumming guitar and frantic drumming that my ears feel like they're vibrating.

The bouncer is right. Most of the girls here look washed up. They're not even trying to seem enthusiastic about whoever's lap they're currently sitting in. I lead us to the bar and order two beers. The barwoman glances between me and Finn with interest. She's got long black hair that almost reaches her ass and black earlobe stretchers that I could poke a finger through. "First time?" she asks in a husky voice as she hands me the bottle.

"Nah. I've been drinking this shit since I was thirteen." I take a long swig as she laughs, eyeing me with what feels like appreciative eyes.

"You've got that sexy lumberjack look about you." So much for the plain clothes.

Finn takes his beer, shifting a little uneasily on his feet. "Amazing what a beard can do."

It's a clever answer that doesn't give her any information about us. I turn to scan the bar, hoping she'll get the hint and move on. I don't see Carter anywhere, but that doesn't mean he's not here.

A blonde in a black dress that's more like a second skin sways past, letting her hand trail over Finn's arm. She's at least forty, so she's almost old enough to be Finn's momma. The older ones always have a soft spot for Finn, like they want to mother him *and* fuck him.

"Hey baby," she says. "You looking for some fun?"

"Not tonight." Finn shoots her a wide smile. "But maybe some other time."

She smiles, but it falters quickly, like she realizes that he's probably not being honest. We both watch her walk away, her ass jiggling with every step. Maybe if we didn't have Skye at home, she might have been worth a try. But there isn't a woman in here that measures up to our woman in any way.

"Hey, West. Is that him?" Finn nods towards a door behind the bar. I turn very slowly, only shooting a fleeting glance in that direction.

Carter Reynolds laughs loudly, sending a shiver of unease up my spine. "Yes."

"There's a woman with him."

"What does she look like?"

"She looks like him. Do you think it's his sister?"

I don't look because I don't want to draw attention to us. "It could be. Does she have a baby with her?"

"Hang on." Finn walks around me, making his way down the bar. I watch as he finds a paper towel and returns. He fake-blows his nose, balls up the tissue, and puts it in his pocket. "There's a baby in a stroller out the back."

"Are you serious?"

"Yeah. It's sleeping through this racket."

"It has to be Hallie." My heart picks up speed, and my neck prickles. We're so close to Skye's stolen child. So close but so far away at the same time.

This is Carter's playground. We're not going to get away with making any moves here. We'll have to find another way to separate that sweet child from this fucked up environment.

"Can you get a picture?" I ask Finn.

"Maybe." He waits until the barwoman is further down the bar, and he follows her to order two more beers. While she's pulling them from the freezer, he holds his phone up,

126

pretending to look at something, using his fingers to mimic swiping as he takes a cover picture. I have no idea if it will be good enough for Skye to see her daughter, but at least he tried.

The second beer slides down as easily as the first. It's been a long and hard week, and I'm grateful for the alcohol and the way it takes the edge off my unease.

"I got some pictures. Shall I send them to Jack now?"

"Do it in the car," I instruct.

Finn nods, shoving his phone into his front pocket. "There are too many people here. Too many obstacles to getting her out." He sounds more like he's trying to convince himself than me. Is he seriously contemplating kidnapping a child in a bar filled with Carter's minions? That is not going to happen, as much as we'd love to make Skye's wish come true.

"There will be another time and place."

"I hope so."

We both watch the black dress woman drape herself all over another young man. She's a cougar, all right.

"This place really is a shithole, isn't it?" I rest my empty bottle down on the bar and wipe the condensation that has dampened my palm on my jeans.

"Sure is."

"Shall we get out of here?"

"Definitely."

I lead the way, checking that Finn is following. I'm bumped by the leather skirt woman who's drunk and staggering toward the ladies room. She gives me a funny look and then carries on.

There's a large group of shaven-headed men by the exit, arguing about something. It's good that we're leaving before anything happens. I squeeze past and draw the cool night air into my lungs, craving the clean alpine scent of my forest.

"Did you get what you came for?" the bouncer asks.

"The beer was good. The pussy, not so much."

He laughs in a raspy way that probably comes from smoking too much. "Told you."

"You did."

When Finn and I are safely in the car and on our way home, I breathe a sigh of relief. This is only the beginning, but at least we know there's a chance to make things right for Skye.

It won't be easy, but we'll do our best.

CHAPTER 16

JACK

DEMONS FROM THE PAST

With West and Finn gone, I'm on edge. Carter Reynolds is a dangerous man with no limits. People have gone missing and had their lives smashed to pieces by him for pettier reasons than Skye's involvement.

It has been years since I last heard his name, and the fact that he's still a player on the scene can only mean that his empire has grown in size and strength. Or his protection racket has.

I hate that I have to be the one who stays with Skye tonight. I want to be out there, investigating, protecting, and taking control. It was my job before Bill fucked it all up.

Despite my insomnia being at its worst this past few weeks, I'm wired and struggle to sit still. I pace the porch, irritating myself with my restlessness. The heat from the fire in the cabin felt stifling, and the stale smell of leftover dinner lingered in the air despite Skye cleaning up after we ate.

I had to get out of there.

Tonight, there is no moon. Stars and distant galaxies twinkle instead, reminding me of how small and insignificant we all are. Troubles linger on the horizon. Troubles that feel huge.

I rest against the railing and close my eyes.

Skye headed to the studio after Finn and West set off on their mission. She didn't want to sit in the cabin, waiting for their return. She needed to keep herself occupied, which is something I understand. As much as I'm curious about what she's doing over there, it suits me to languish in my solitude. At least from here, I can make sure she's safe.

The recent wind has died away, and this evening is still. The only sound I hear is my ragged breath as I shudder against the dropping temperature. The thought of smashing up some wood passes through my mind, but I also have to keep an eye on the studio and the cabin after Ethan's latest visit. Although he's a pathetic weasel, I doubt that Skye could do much to protect herself if she found herself alone with him.

Closing my eyes, I imagine myself lighting up a cigarette and inhaling deeply on the welcome tang of nicotine, and the sudden rush of calm hits me full-on. But that is something I managed to bury well in the past, and that is where I intend it to stay. The last time I had a drag on a cigarette, it was one that belonged to Bill.

He never worried about vices. He was into them all despite being a cop.

A bright flash of rage surges within me as the memory of our last job together resurfaces: Bill inside, getting his fix, me outside, keeping guard. It was stupid. The undercover operation was in full flow, and we had watched the joint all evening. Bill somehow escaped from a rear exit unseen, making his way back out front as backup arrived.

The son of a bitch set me up and had his drug dealing felons inside testify that the bent copper cutting a deal was me. It was lucky I had some dirt on a high-ranking officer that I threatened to expose, or I would have ended up banged up instead of out on my ear with a payoff.

Bill Tappin didn't get to his high rank through being a decent cop but by knowing the right people inside and outside the force, and being prepared to do whatever it took to survive.

He knows Carter Reynolds.

I flex my hands into fists, trying to keep my rage at bay, but I have to admit defeat.

I stomp down the wooden steps that are slick with moisture and head off into the forest, grabbing West's tomahawk as I go.

I know exactly what I'm going to do.

Not far in, there is a clearing where we store bigger logs, perfect for smashing the crap out of to ward off a fucking stress-induced aneurysm.

I tear off my jacket and toss it aside in one rapid move.

I haul the biggest log out from under the tarp. It's huge and weighty and carries a strong scent of cedar. I throw the ax high and then bring it smashing down. The sound reverberates, sending birds flapping from the trees around me and something scuttling through the undergrowth. I do it again, hitting the same spot, pleased at my precision.

Too hot, I unbutton my shirt and toss it with my coat. I inhale one huge breath to fill my lungs and hold it for as long as possible, lifting my gaze into the navy-blue sky.

I swing the ax and bring it down repeatedly until sweat drips down my spine and heat rises from my skin. A fierce burning in my muscles and the release of pent-up fury does nothing to slow me. Only when the huge log splinters into two huge chunks do I rest the ax head against the ground and pant in relief.

Sweat trickles between my pecs and abdominals, cooling in the chilled air. This is what I need to tip the balance back to a point where I can function. I listen out, hearing nothing but silence around me. Whatever Skye is doing in the studio is quiet.

I continue my frenzied chopping, losing track of time until I almost run out of logs to smash. My thoughts start to calm, and my racing pulse evens out. My swings become less powerful, and I see the destruction that I've wrought.

My mind is clear, and I know what I need to do.

I thrust my hand into my pocket and take out my phone, tapping in a number that I haven't used for years but is etched into my mind with a permanent marker. I exhale and keep my voice low. It rings twice, then goes straight to voicemail. Perfect. Leaving a voicemail will be better than speaking to him directly.

Hello Bill. It's me. It's been a while. How are you? I see you've done well. Moved through the ranks. Good for you.

I've been doing some thinking about our days on the force when we were partners. Got me thinking about how sometimes we've just got to redress the balance. You know? Put wrong things right. Repay favors.

I've had a few flashbacks recently. Remembering those times is hitting me hard, Bill. I ended up leaving with my tail between my legs back then and now I see this. Deputy Chief of Police, Bill Tappin!

I wonder how it would look if things from the past came back to haunt us. I don't suppose that would look too good for you, Bill.

Anyway, give my love to Darcy and the boys. I hope they're well. I haven't settled down myself just yet.

Things I need to deal with first.

Be good to hear from you. I have the same number, Bill. Get in touch.

I hang up. There is no need to leave my name. He'll know it's me.

And he owes me. There is no doubting it. I covered his ass and ended up out on mine.

He never owned up, and I wasn't going to beat him, so we left it buried where I'm sure he hoped, and maybe prayed, it would stay.

I'd love to be a fly on the wall when he hits playback on my message.

I used to want to exact some kind of revenge, but that feeling left me when I used the payout I received to move into this beautiful forest. I found my place in the world because of Bill's betrayal.

Every experience puts us on a path; even the ones we prefer never happened.

Now, I don't wish the man any harm, but I'm prepared to come out of the shadows so he can pay his debt and help Skye. At the very least, he can dig around to see what Carter Reynolds has been up to behind the scenes and what kind of a threat he is to Skye now.

But I really want protection from any repercussions in our dealings with Carter. And perhaps what he ultimately owes me, a total cover-up. They say it's who you know, not what you know. I reckon it's both of those things.

Now all I can do is wait. Wait and see if he will do what he should. The very act of reaching out to him after all this time will be enough for him to know that I'm not playing games. I may have kept his secrets in the past, but they can be resurrected if he doesn't play ball.

I push the phone back into my pocket and dress before I head back. As I round the corner, I notice that Finn and West are back. The truck is parked at a funny angle tonight.

I shouldn't have left Skye in the barn for so long while my mind was distracted.

Quickening my pace, my pulse intensifies, and I stride towards the porch, almost tearing the door from its hinges in my hurry to be updated.

West, Finn, and Skye all look up at the sudden disturbance, their mouths agape.

"Everything okay?" West asks.

I give him a determined nod, and he immediately carries on showing Skye something on his phone. Skye is slumped forward, flicking through the screen. She gasps, taking her hands to her face, and stifled sobs escape in response to whatever she's seeing.

Finn is pouring shots of JD but gives up halfway to comfort Skye. She seems oblivious to his presence and alone in her agony. He returns to the shots and passes Skye one, urging her to drink for medicinal purposes.

She downs the shot, gasping at the bitter heat.

"You really saw her?"

West nods. "Finn took the photos. We couldn't get any closer without arousing suspicion. I'm sorry, Skye."

She shakes her head. "This is more than I could have hoped for. I know she's alive. That's more than I've known for weeks."

"Is your friend the woman behind the bar with the black hair and those things in her ears?"

"No. Shona doesn't look like that."

Skye slumps against the back of her chair, breathing hard. Her hand clasps at her throat and she makes a strangled sound as her breaths get shorter and shallower.

"Skye?" Finn steps forward, but I'm quicker to respond. I scoop her into my arms, pulling her against my chest. "It's okay, Skye. You're okay. Hallie's going to be okay. Just breathe." I inhale a long and loud breath, hold it for a second, then exhale it equally slowly. "Copy my breathing, yeah?"

Her eyes focus on mine, and she tries to mimic my pace, failing at first but then gradually matching the slow pull and push of my diaphragm.

Finn and West watch and exchange glances that I don't try to analyze. Skye opens her eyes, looking up at me. I pull her in for a tight embrace, and she tries to wriggle free feebly but then accepts defeat. Her eyes are wet with tears, which soak through my shirt as she eventually rests herself against me, trying to sink into me as much as she can.

She may not find comfort in my dark heart, but she will find protection.

"Can one of you get her some water?" I growl.

I want to know what happened tonight, but I need Skye ready and able to tell us what and who features in these photos that Finn and West have plenty of.

I carry her back to the kitchen table and place her in a chair. Finn rests the water in front of her, but she doesn't notice. I push it closer to her hand. "Drink, Skye."

On autopilot, she grasps the glass and downs the cool liquid all in one go. Her body shivers as it passes through her, but it seems to revive her a little.

West pulls out the phone again, and she continues to look.

We all watch Skye inhaling every detail of her daughter through the photos. There is one picture in particular that she keeps going back to.

"Can you tell us who else is in the pictures?"

She ignores my questions and continues flicking through just the baby pictures. I understand her fixation, but we can't let her dwell. She's in danger of losing a grip on the reason behind West and Finn's visit to Carter's bar.

The fire roars in the background as if it is in tune with the panic and stress that are clearly taking hold of Skye. Suddenly she drops the phone and shoves the chair back, standing only to brace her hands on her knees and gasp for breath all over again.

"Sit down, for Christ's sake, Skye!" I can't help myself. We don't have time to keep reviving her, and all this desperate energy is raising my blood pressure all over again. I'm going to need to chop more wood.

"It's Shona!"

"Shona?"

"The woman I was telling you about, Jack. The one who I reached out to and messaged the other night! It's her in this photo, holding Hallie. And looking too damn cozy with Carter. I don't understand."

Silence follows as we all consider the implications of this new information.

The message Skye sent to Shona could give Carter enough information for him to find her here.

Maybe she didn't tell him. We can't know for sure.

But either way, we need to be prepared for the worst.

I want to avoid discussing this part in front of Skye. She's dealing with enough as it is. What she needs is a warm embrace in bed so she can fall asleep feeling secure. I'm about to encourage Finn to take her so I can talk things over with West when the sound of shattered glass ricochets all around us, and a sudden gust of cutting night air bursts into the room like an unexpected explosion.

Something smashes into the TV behind us all, and we react, crouching to protect ourselves initially, but instinct drives us all to shelter Skye, and she's pushed behind the wall that we all make with our bodies as we try to work out what the hell has happened.

"What the fuck?" West sprints to the front door, yanking it open. I'm two seconds behind. We eye the shattered window before craning our necks to stare into the darkness. The trees rustle, and a bird calls in the distance, but there is no one visible and no footsteps to reveal the attacker.

Finn emerges, holding a large rock that could have killed one of us if we were unlucky enough to be standing in the firing line. This doesn't have the hallmark of a gangster, no matter how small-time Carter is. This has the cowardice of Ethan written all over it.

"Carter?" Finn asks.

I shake my head. "Trust me. Men like him don't throw stones."

"Damn. Ethan?" West is on the same page as me. He

would know. A man this desperate needs to be careful. He's unwittingly getting himself tangled up in some very messy business. West storms into the darkness, uncaring that he's not wearing shoes or a coat to protect him from the elements. I don't follow him because I know Ethan's running away faster than we can follow.

"I'm going to get some boards to hammer over this damned window. Let's get something happening here. And for God's sake, we need to get Skye to bed. This day needs to be over."

Finn follows me out to get tools and board and walk the perimeter. Ethan might be a coward, but I want to ensure he's not persistent.

When West returns, confirming what I already suspected, he disappears inside to make sure Skye gets the rest she needs.

We make quick work of fixing up the window, and there isn't any trace of an intruder around the lodge. Finn and I stare into the forest on every side, finding nothing but gently swaying trees.

"Ethan's becoming a problem," Finn says.

"Ethan's always been a problem, but it's one we can fix."

He nods, understanding what I mean. We've let this go for too long, feeling sorry for him rather than putting him in his place. It's left West looking guilty for something he's innocent of and Ethan thinking he's a bigger man than he is. It's time for all of that to change.

Back inside where it's still stiflingly warm, I keep my boots on in case Ethan comes back for a second shot. I take off my shirt and sit in just my worn jeans. The mood is somber as we all take a seat around the table.

"What happened at the bar?"

West speaks first.

"Carter's bar is a fucking dive, full of the lowest elements. We couldn't wait to get the hell out."

"Definitely no place for an innocent child like Hallie."

Finn shakes his head and folds his lips.

"What the hell was Skye doing getting mixed up in a world like that?"

I shut West down. We haven't got time for analyzing anyone's past mistakes. All we can work with is what we have now. "We don't know if Carter knows Skye's whereabouts. And now you two have walked among his fucking community, we are committed to dealing with this. It isn't just about Skye and Hallie anymore. Our whole damn livelihood is at stake here."

We let this thought settle, and none of us notices that Skye is back in the hallway, leaning against the wall for support as if even holding her own body upright is an impossible task right now, until her small voice cuts through the silence.

"I'm sorry. I really am. I don't know what else to say!" Her voice seems to come from far away and fades into nothingness.

"You don't need to apologize." Finn is on his feet and lumbers towards her, ready to comfort the girl who can't sleep. He leads her back to her room and doesn't return.

"I called Bill," I tell West. "He didn't pick up, but I left a message that he will respond to."

"Let me know what he says."

I nod and lean against the chair, cracking my back on the wood.

The events of this evening have wiped me out, and the familiar sense of foreboding that accompanies my exhaustion and wired emotions threatens to spill over the edges of my mind.

"You should go to bed," I tell West. "I'll keep watch. Set an alarm for three am. You can take the second shift."

As West leaves the room, I pull my rifle from the cupboard, making sure it's loaded.

I sit with it over my knee and pull my phone from my pocket.

One new message.

My pulse quickens, and my chest tightens. But as I listen, my blood seems to leave my body, and all around me, there is only stillness.

And then the entire world comes crashing down around me. I'm frozen in time.

And I can do nothing.

It takes every ounce of my restraint to stay still, to not tear out into the night to torture the wrong target, to destroy everything in my path.

That wouldn't be the way to redress the balance.

And right now, I need to keep my cool for Skye. For West and Finn.

And for me, because God knows that dropping dead from a cardiac arrest would be damn inconvenient right now.

It's not the message I anticipated, but more life-shattering than I could ever imagine.

That son of bitch stepfather of mine chooses today to drop dead.

Before I had a chance to find him and exact my revenge.

And he left me as his next of kin.

Son of a bitch.

CHAPTER 17

WEST

PICTURES AND PAIN

Skye has to come to work with us every day. Leaving her behind isn't safe. It doesn't feel that safe to ask her to hang out at a hazardous site with rough lumberjacks, but at least we're around to deal with any danger that might come about.

On Monday, she tries to read to pass the time but admits she finds concentrating a challenge.

On Tuesday morning, Jack installs her in the trailer cabin that doubles as our break room with a book and a sketch pad that will hopefully keep her occupied all day. Her phone must remain off since she potentially compromised it with the message.

Ethan calls in sick, which is a good thing. If I see him today, I don't think I'd be able to hold off punching him in his stupid face. I used to feel so much guilt for what happened with his brother, but his actions have turned that guilt into exasperation and now into burning anger. Skye has enough on her plate without worrying about getting killed by a rock flying through the window.

My hard hat makes my scalp itch, but I work through it, focusing on the giant tree we're taking down next.

Aiden is working with me. He's a good guy and an old hand. I trust him to make decisions that won't put either of us in danger.

We're almost done when Liam emerges from the tree line, pulling off his gloves and watching the mighty Western Red Cedar fall hard enough to shake the ground.

I tip my head questioningly in Liam's direction, and he urges me closer. "Everything okay?" Maybe something has happened with Skye.

"Last night, there were some new people at the bar … I thought I should let you know."

"Who?"

"He didn't say, but I overheard one of his friends calling him Carter. He said he was looking for a girl called Skye. That's the woman you have living with you, right?"

"What else did he say?"

"There were a lot of them, throwing their weight around. It got messy."

"Messy, how?"

Liam grins and rubs his hand over his red beard, dislodging bark that was wedged in the dense hair. "We made them leave. They didn't like it, but those city boys think they can come into our town and make threats against our friends. The Shadow Outlaws were there last night, too. When I told them that Skye was with Finn, they ran those guys out of town."

I grit my teeth and peel off my gloves. Aiden calls out, already moving onto our next tree target, but I can't focus on logging when danger seems to be creeping closer with every minute that passes. "Thanks for telling me and for getting those assholes out of our neighborhood."

"What are friends for?" He runs his finger under the

rim of his hard hat as he eyes the tree we felled. "So, who are they?"

"Bad news," I say. "That's all you need to know. If it happens again, can you call me? It doesn't matter how late."

"Sure. But I doubt they'll be back. We made it clear they're not welcome around here."

"Oh, they'll be back, and next time, they won't listen to anything anyone says. They know they're close to their target. They'll only try harder."

"They want to take Skye?"

I nod. I'm not going to fill Liam in on the Hallie situation. "Carter's her ex-husband."

He shifts his feet, widening his stance. "Jesus, West. You stumbled into something messy with her. I hope she's worth it."

"She is," I say before I can think, but then it hits me. Defending her isn't just about the instinct to protect a woman in need. It isn't about protecting what's mine because I paid for her fair and square. It's about wanting Skye to be safe with her daughter. It's about the desire to keep her with us after the contract has expired.

"Then you call us if you need to, okay? Men like that don't belong around women. They don't belong around here, either."

His support isn't surprising—Liam's good people. But feeling part of a broader community that will stand by me and mine in times of trouble takes me back to my service days when I knew my brothers had my back. There's a lot about those days I'd rather forget, but not that part.

"Thanks, man."

He nods, beginning to tug his thick work gloves back on his hands. As Aiden calls me again, eager to hit our quota, the forest swallows Liam's retreating form.

At lunchtime, we all meet to check on Skye. She's quick to close her sketchpad as soon as she sees us, but Jack snatches it from her hand and leafs through it, even as she struggles to get it back.

"Wow." His mouth drops open and his eyes bulge, but when he shows me what he's looking at, I see why he's surprised. She's sketched us from memory; three faces staring off the page on a background of looming trees. It's like looking at myself in the mirror, except I'm in grayscale. Somehow, she's managed to capture Finn's kind eyes and Jack's fiercely gritted jaw. She's got my wariness, too.

"That's really good," I tell her as she slumps back into her chair, resigned to us seeing what she's been working on.

Finn flops down next to Skye and throws his arm around her shoulder, pulling her closer so he can kiss the top of her head. She blushes sweetly and pulls away, looking around like she's conscious of the public display. She begins to root around in the large cool pack she brought with her this morning, passing out foil-wrapped sandwiches and pouring cups of steaming soup from a thermos. Jack eventually returns her drawings, taking on a thoughtful expression. Something about her choosing to draw us has touched him, even though he'd never admit it.

The soup is spicy tomato filled with soft peppers and shredded chicken. It's delicious and perfect to warm us from the inside out. Despite the worry that's nagging at Skye, she smiles when we compliment her cooking and even laughs out loud when we all groan in pleasure at the delicious homemade chocolate brownies she made for dessert. When our colleagues look over jealously, she pulls out a large plastic container and hands it around. If the men in this place were wary about her being here today, they quickly change their minds.

"She's a keeper," Liam jokes, but the wink he gives me after tells me he means what he says.

I know she is.

I feel it in my bones. If we can just get her baby back, I can see exactly what kind of woman she'll be—the kind of woman who'll fit perfectly into our lives. We can grow together, twisting and turning like the ivy on the trees outside.

"So, Skye, you wanna draw me?" Liam tilts his face from side to side, displaying his profile.

"I don't have a sheet of paper big enough," Skye jokes. All the lumberjacks dissolve into laughter, including Jack, who seems to see her with new eyes, smiling softly as she shines brightly. He helps her gather the trash and even gets up to toss it in the can in the corner. And then, shock of all shocks, he offers to make Skye coffee. The open-mouthed faces in the place are fucking hilarious.

My mom always told me that people have the power to change each other. I always thought she meant for the worst, but watching Jack soften because of Skye, and Finn smile like his face is going to crack, is a beautiful thing to witness.

After work is over, I drive us all back to the lodge. Skye waits with me while Jack and Finn circle the place and check inside. As soon as we confirm the coast is clear, we make our way up the wooden steps. Skye hangs her coat on a hook by the door next to Finn and Jack's. I add mine there, too, and the sight of our clothes together is so homey that I have to head to the sink and fix myself a glass of water to swallow away the ache in my throat.

Skye disappears into her room, and Finn comes back after his shower to tell us he can hear her crying.

Jack stares towards the door to the hallway as though he wants to comfort her but doesn't know how. We're all walking on eggshells.

He pours himself half a glass of Jack and slumps into a chair next to the empty fireplace. He knocks back the whole glass of liquor and then clears his throat noisily. "He died."

"Who? I ask.

"My stepfather."

Shit. This isn't a straightforward passing where people feel grief over their loss. This is a fucked up, complicated passing of a man who caused a lot of pain. "When."

"Yesterday."

"How do you feel?" Finn asks. He's brave. I wouldn't have approached that part so directly.

"Like I want to find his corpse and hack it into pieces, then piss on them." He laughs, but it's not warm. It's dark and hollow and filled with malice.

Finn rubs his hand over his chin, rasping the stubble there. He picks up the bottle of Jack Daniels and pours two more glasses, then tops up Jack's glass.

"To Jack's evil stepdad. May he rot in hell and suffer all of the hurt he inflicted on others."

Jack stares at Finn, and for a second, I think he'll fly across the room and tear his head from his neck. Instead, he raises his glass and drinks. "Rot in hell," he repeats.

"Rot in hell," Finn and I say in unison.

"Have you heard from Bill yet?" I ask.

Jack shakes his head. "He'll call. And I'll be ready when he does."

Then Jack does something I never thought I'd see. He heads over to the fridge and starts to rustle up a meal for us all, leaving Skye to rest and grieve her pain in private.

CHAPTER 18

FINN

BLOWN IN THE WIND

The tension from the past few days is taking its toll. Jack's recent confession and subsequent considerate behavior feel like a cause for concern, especially against the backdrop of his disheveled appearance. It's just so out of character to offer to make Skye coffee in front of the guys in the yard and then make dinner.

I always worry that he will tip over the edge. He never does. At least he hasn't since I've known him.

He usually lets off steam by hacking logs to pieces.

I worry that his current kindness is concealing something too dark to even contemplate.

Skye is restless, getting more desperate by the day. She has lost weight, and her clothes are noticeably looser, hanging from her slight frame. Her pallor and worried eyes tell me she's not sleeping enough, and her cheekbones seem hollower than when she arrived. Last night, I held her in bed, but I was exhausted and fell asleep before she did. When I woke, she was already up.

West is the only one of us who seems to be in control of himself with the current situation.

He's on a mission to keep us all safe and together, plotting and planning. His eyes move quickly, and his face remains impassive. The usual wariness he wears like a cloak is magnified.

I know he feels bolstered by the boys at the lumberyard and my friends from the biker crew having our backs. Even the founder, Bones, has offered his total support.

That doesn't change how he feels, though.

With Ethan and Carter both moving closer, we're all on high alert.

West stays at the cabin today. Skye's in a state and none of us feel like leaving her alone, day or night. We are taking no risks and are routinely bolting all doors and windows no matter how short a time we leave the cabin for. The curtains are permanently drawn.

West keeps his gun by his side around the clock, something he's never done, and Jack's is never too far away.

The yard is busy as demand always seems to peak this time of year.

To be honest, me and Jack could do with the distraction and although I've been at the yard a few hours, I've not yet laid eyes on Jack.

He was up and out with the dawn chorus.

The mood amongst the guys in the yard is somber. We're all feeling the pressure as well as the threat.

But we're hypervigilant.

Ethan is back, but he's keeping his head down and working at a remote site on the fringe of the forest where there is less chance of him annoying the hell out of anyone else. His shady vibe has no place amongst the good guys here, but we're forced to tolerate him because, despite his obvious weaknesses, he's a decent lumberjack, and recruiting staff is not easy task. His family has worked the forests in these parts for generations, and history and connections go a long way in this business.

We all have a stake in the forest.

I've earned mine on merit and association rather than bloodline.

This is something that me, Jack, and West all have in common.

Just before noon, the rumble of a truck rounding the tree line and pulling into the lot outside the trailer cabin draws my attention.

It's Jack.

I put down my tools to greet him as he emerges from the cab.

"Meet me in the trailer in five." Jack seems more energized somehow, and there is a glint in his eye before he strides with purpose and confidence towards the trailer.

None of the other guys will be here until lunch at one, so we'll have time to discuss in private.

The trailer door swings shut, and with that, I return to my tools and clear them away.

Jack has made coffee and is standing on watch at the rear window as I enter the trailer. His body is twitchy, and his nervous energy is palpable.

Hearing me enter, he turns and pushes a steaming mug across to the place where I sit.

"It's sorted with Bill. We've spoken. It's all going ahead."

I let his words sink in. It explains Jack's change of demeanor. He must have been with Bill this morning. It is why he hasn't been at the yard. And he's clearly pleased with the outcome, empowered almost.

"So what's the plan, Jack?" He pauses for a few moments, but I see that he's processing how much he wants to tell me. It's what he'll keep to himself that will worry me the most.

"Whatever happens, there will be no repercussions for

us. Carter and his men will be going away for a long time. Maybe forever if we get lucky. But we are free to set them up, lure them here, and then make sure that they never hurt Skye or anyone else ever again."

"Have you seen Bill? Where did you meet?"

Jack shakes his head. "No, he wouldn't meet me face to face. He's chicken shit. But he called early this morning, and I've been out getting the plan straight in my mind. I know what needs to happen, and we need to check a few more sites, speak to a few people, and tighten up my plan."

"I need to know what's going to happen, Jack. I need things straight in my mind."

"Finn, you need to trust me. Have I ever let you down?"

"No. Never. But what if Carter brings more trouble than we anticipate?"

Jack's cell begins to ring, and he pulls it out of his shirt pocket, selects the loudspeaker, and rests it on the table between us.

"Jack?"

"Yes, it's me. What we were talking about the other day … are you in?"

"Course, Jack. You know it. We are all in. I've spoken to the boys, and we've got your backs; just say when." Nathan's voice is instantly recognizable, deep, and gravelly. He's the biggest of all the lumberjacks and the only one who surpasses me in size and bulk.

Jack gave him a chance and hired him when no one else would.

We both feel we owe Jack.

"Thanks." With that, Jack cuts the call and drops his phone back into his pocket. "We've got the Shadows and the yard crew on our side. Reggie is in after Carter was sniffing around his daughters in the bar. I need you to trust me that I'll figure out the rest so there are no repercussions, whatever happens."

I nod, but I'm still not sure. I have a bad feeling that

Jack's personal craving for revenge is lurking behind this plan, as though he can quench his pain by focusing on Carter and his treatment of Skye. Where Nathan has a wife and child to keep him on the straight and narrow, Jack isn't anchored. And with his stepfather's death coming out of the blue, I have a feeling that he's focusing on this as a way of avenging the past when he had no control.

Through Skye, he's attempting to cut out old tissue.

All I can do is listen and support the guy I love as if he was my brother.

And work with him to protect our woman from harm.

"Get what you need. We're heading off-site for now. Ron Maggs has agreed to it. I went to see him this morning. The others have got this, and we've got family troubles that need our attention. Priorities. It's all about priorities. And you need to get in touch with the Outlaws. Get Bones to give me a call." My stomach flips, and I'm not sure if it's fear or excitement, but I get the sense that something has been set in motion, and it's only going to speed up from this point towards a conclusion that will make us or break us.

Despite it only being early afternoon, the light outside is dim, and gray clouds gather overhead with an accompanying wind that makes the trees rustle and creak. I walk next to Jack from the truck, eyes scanning left and right. Jack keeps his hands in his pockets and his eyes firmly forward.

Looking over my shoulder, I can't shake the feeling that we're being watched.

It's just paranoia, but I haven't had to watch my back since I left the streets, and it is not something that I want to have to do again.

Supporting Jack is the only way to get our way of life back.

At the cabin, I ensure every bolt is firmly in place before removing my coat and boots. West is making up the fire out of necessity; the air has a bite to it, and we want to keep Skye warm and safe. His gun rests against the mantelpiece like a guard standing to attention.

Jack slumps silently into the armchair, watching West work, his long legs sprawled out before him. He clutches his rifle between his meaty hands, ready for anything, even in a relaxed pose.

Skye is fast asleep on the sofa, a blanket pulled up to her chin, but a tight expression etched onto her pale face. She's not finding rest even when sleeping.

"Bill called this morning." Jack cuts the silence, and West snaps his head around.

"Bill? He finally came good?"

Jack smirks, and West heads to the cabinet for the Jack Daniels.

I'm about to pull up a chair when there is a muffled tapping at the door.

I'm the only one who seems to notice, and moments later, the sound rises to a knock, and we are all alerted. It is accompanied by a sense of urgency.

Even Skye sits up suddenly, her blanket falling to the floor.

She looks exposed and vulnerable, dressed in nothing but a plaid shirt; one of West's.

West strides forward, but I'm already ahead of him. I move towards the front door with West at my shoulder. Jack stands and moves slowly behind us, the click of his gun cutting the air.

Sliding back the bolts and pulling open the door more confidently than I feel, I recognize the woman standing on our porch, framed by the gray light behind her.

It is the woman from the other night. The one from the photo that got Skye all riled up. Shona? That's it.

She looks much younger out of the bar setting, wide-eyed, almost feline.

The blue woolen hat she's wearing sits low as if she's trying to disguise herself as well as defend herself from the elements. Shadows under her eyes tell of sleepless nights. She has the same haunted look that Skye had the first night we met her.

Damn this Carter guy. What the hell does he do to these women?

Her eyes dart from side to side, and she jerks her neck to glance behind her as if she may have been followed.

The tension radiating from her is tangible, and I instinctively stand aside to allow her in and slam and bolt the door immediately behind her.

She shuffles hastily into the main body of the cabin, taking in West's and my mighty bulk before freezing on the spot when she sets eyes on Skye.

Skye's expression is a mixture of shock, anger, relief, and something else. Confusion maybe?

Jack approaches, and for a moment, the only sound is the pulsing in my ears.

Her eyes widen at the sight of Jack's gun.

"I didn't know what else to do." Her voice is almost a whisper; she's choking back tears, and Skye is frozen in place.

"How the hell did you know where to find us? Does he know you're here?" Jack growls, and the harshness of his tone catches our visitor off guard.

Shona takes a step back until she's pressed against the door, with her hands spread against the wood. Her frail build shrinks further, and her eyes dart around the room.

"I had to come," she says. "Please." One of her hands rises slowly and she focuses on Jack, waiting for him to lower his gun. When he doesn't, she blinks and then removes her hat, which somehow expresses her vulnerability. Skye rises and crosses the room, putting her body between the long barrel of the rifle and Shona.

Jack immediately lowers the gun, but his expression is far from relaxed.

Shona trembles before dissolving into sobs that wrack her body. She seems wrung out. Skye steps closer and wraps her arms around Shona, and the woman sinks into the embrace, her face lost in Skye's neck.

Skye keeps her head level, staring straight ahead. The embrace is stiff, the impact of the photos of Shona with Carter and Hallie the other night still resting between them.

"Hallie misses you, Skye. She's safe, but she misses you. And I do, too. I'm so sorry, Skye. So sorry." She clings to Skye's shirt desperately.

Does she know that we've seen the photos giving her away? Why has she come here?

Jack shifts until he's to the left of Shona, raising his gun again. She glances at him, and pulls back from Skye, focusing on the two barrels of the gun.

"Why are you here?" His voice is a menacing growl.

"Carter doesn't know, but I had to come. I told him I was staying a night or two with a friend. I didn't know where to go. I overheard Carter talking about Reggies's bar, and when I got into town, I met someone at the gas station, who told me where to find you. I think his name was Ethan?"

West growls, which takes Shona by surprise, and she shrinks back in shock. "God damn it. That fucking useless piece of fucking shit. He'll get us all fucking killed."

"You said Carter doesn't know that you're here. But does he know that I am?" Skye's voice has a hint of desperation, but she's trying to keep herself composed.

Shona casts her eyes down again, the shadows beneath them deep and dark. "He doesn't know exactly where … yet."

I step forward, drawing her attention. "I saw you the other night. You and Carter. Looking cozy. And with Hallie, too."

Shona sniffs as fresh tears break her attempts to compose herself.

"I was taken in, Skye. I'm so sorry. After you left, he made a play for me. You know how he is, throwing his cash around, indulging me, making me feel special. Until it became obvious that he used me to get to you. He took my phone. He read your message. Then everything changed."

Skye slowly lifts her gaze and silently addresses each one of us in turn. Her eyes are pleading with us to say or do something.

"He's angry, Skye. So angry. I didn't know how bad he was ... I never saw what you saw, not really." Her voice trails to a whisper. "He's not going to rest until ..."

She doesn't finish the sentence, but we all know what remains unsaid.

He's coming for Skye. He wants to finish what he started once and for all.

"What about Hallie? Where is she?" Skye sobs.

Shona shakes her head. "I was caring for her, but when Carter found the message, he took her away ... to his sister's maybe. I overheard him telling her that she'll need to travel ... I think he's planning to get Hallie out of the country for a while."

Tears leak from Skye's eyes, but she swipes them away and turns to me, then West and finally Jack with pleading eyes.

Help me, they say. *Help me get my baby back.*

She won't ask us outright, but every fiber of her being strains to express her desperation.

Jack moves forward, seating himself at the table and resting his gun across the polished wood. He takes a shot of Jack Daniels and tosses it back. He taps his cellphone, and the sound of a dial tone on the loudspeaker moves to a calling tone. Moments later, the call is answered, a gruff cough being the only indication of this.

"It's me." Jack's voice is low, steady, and strong.

Whoever Jack called is listening only.

"We can't wait. It has to be brought forward.

Tomorrow. See what you can do."

The sound of someone inhaling deeply and then breathing out audibly is evident on the line.

The tension is clear.

"Leave it with me." The call is cut dead.

Jack sits still with his eyes closed. Eventually, he surveys us all and reaching one beefy arm around to grip the back of his neck, he fixes his gaze on me and growls.

"Give me Liam's number." Gripped by emotional and physical exhaustion, Skye and Shona move to the couch. Shona pulls out her phone to show Skye pictures of Hallie, but Jack snatches it and turns it off, then searches it for a tracking device, which he doesn't find.

"You can't leave," he says. "Not until this thing is resolved."

Shona nods, and Skye stands abruptly like she has suddenly realized what 'resolved' means.

This situation will come to a head, and the cards will fall.

We need to eat, so I rustle up some pasta with a ready-made sauce, hoping quick and filling will be enough. Skye helps me, running on a kind of dazed autopilot as she slowly grates cheese, staring into the middle distance.

Jack disappears for more hushed conversations. Now Shona is in our midst; we can't speak openly.

Afterward, Jack offers to sleep on the armchair with his gun resting across his body. I know his priority is making sure Shona doesn't flee into the night.

He wants her where he can keep his eyes on her.

Skye finds a blanket for Shona and hovers in the kitchen.

"I'll sleep with you tonight," West tells her, fixing himself some water and offering some to Skye.

Skye touches my arm, and I pull her into my chest, feeling her sink against me. Her tiny frame feels so fragile, like a bird that's fallen to the earth, all its delicate bones fractured.

155

"I'm sorry," she whispers. "Sorry that I've stolen your peace."

I stoop to kiss the top of her head. The scent of almonds and something sweet is familiar to me now, and she grips me tighter.

"I can't do this without you." Her voice is a whisper.

"You've got us, Skye. You're not alone. You'll never be alone."

Moments pass until we break away from each other. She pads slowly across the room to stand before Jack. He doesn't let go of the gun as she bends to kiss his lips. I imagine him turning away from such gentle affection, embarrassed to show this side of him in front of us, but he doesn't. His eyes drift closed as Skye's hand rests against the messy rasp of his beard. "Jack."

Just the soft murmur of his name communicates so much.

West carries his gun in one hand and moves to take Skye's hand in the other. He leads her from the room, and the creak of the wooden floorboards tracks their retreat. Eventually, the door to her room clicks shut.

Jack nods a simple goodnight, and I scan Shona, finding her staring at me with wide, fearful eyes.

She's not a foe, but she's also not a friend.

I'm wary that she might be a honey trap, and it's evident from the way Jack has his gun aimed just above her head that he feels the same.

I decide that I need to be armed, so I load the spare rifle from the gun cupboard. Back in my room, the chill in the air grips me tightly, and I grab an extra shirt, pulling it firmly around me.

I tug the curtain aside, staring into the inky blackness. For the first time in a long time, the expanse of the forest outside gives me shivers, like a cloak concealing a thousand pairs of eyes. The cabin, which has always felt like a haven, a home, now feels like the target of some deep-rooted hatred, revenge, and intent.

It is just a matter of time until the whole thing implodes.

Jerking the curtains shut, I return to take my place next to Jack. We've been a team for as long as we've known each other through whatever has come our way. It'll always be like that. He lowers his chin in acknowledgment and then closes his eyes. I hope he can rest a little easier knowing I'm by his side.

Despite the thoughts that linger in every corner of my mind and a creeping sense of dread, increasing waves of exhaustion take over my body, pulling me into an ocean of vivid dreams of past times that can never be resurrected. Of another little girl out there in the world who'll never be found.

CHAPTER 19

SKYE

A WING AND A PRAYER

Everybody in my life has let me down at some point. My parents cut me off when I made choices they disagreed with. My friends drifted away when Carter became a controlling presence in my life. Carter pretended to be one person, then morphed into another when I was at my most vulnerable. Shona, who I thought was my friend, was quick to fill the space I left in Carter's bed and in my daughter's life.

There isn't a person in the world who's proven themselves to be loyal.

Yet three men are risking everything for me, and I don't understand why.

I should be nothing to them.

They bought me at an auction, like a car or a piece of furniture. A convenience to make their lives easier. But they keep me between them like they're a security detail protecting a head of state. They hold me while I cry and rest with me during my fitful hours of sleep. They secretly make plans to help find Hallie and put the two halves of my heart back together.

It's terrifying because I promised I wouldn't let anyone in again. It was the only way I could force myself into this year-long arrangement. Trusting takes too much strength, and I'm weak.

So fucking weak.

But they're strong.

West is like a block of granite. There's nothing that can break his resolve. Finn is a trunk of hardwood. The sun, the wind, and the rain don't penetrate. Jack is a black diamond, hard enough to etch steel and too dark to see to the heart of.

Next to them, I feel as vulnerable as a baby mouse, reliant on them for food and warmth, close to getting consumed by a predator at any second.

"Don't worry. Everything's under control," West tells me as he watches me dress. His eyes on me aren't sexual. They're concerned. I'm thinner, and it makes me look breakable.

Even last night, when I wrapped myself around him, feeling needy and wanting him to make me forget, he whispered that I needed sleep, and held himself back with restraint I didn't know he possessed.

West has his rifle in his hand, but it doesn't bother me. That's how sure I am that none of them will ever hurt me.

They've chosen to go into battle for me and my child, who they've never met.

They'll fight my enemy and reclaim what's mine, and all I can do is hope, pray, and wait.

It's the waiting that's killing me slowly, piece by pathetic piece.

I focus on West's rugged face; his chiseled cheekbones, and the lines etched around his intense, dark eyes give him an air of maturity that inspires a sense of trust.

"I've never held a gun before," I say, eyeing the small pistol that rests on my bed.

"All you need to do is point and shoot." Easy for him to say.

I rub between my brows, trying to erase the tension that's bunching every muscle in my body.

West, seeing my anxiety, softens. "All we need you to do is ensure Shona doesn't blow this whole thing. *That* will guarantee she doesn't open her mouth at the wrong time." His eyes focus on my fingers that rest against the cool metal and then wrap around the handle, testing its weight again.

"This is going to work?" It's half statement, half question. I trust them, but I need to know they believe in themselves.

"There is never just one route out of a difficult situation, Skye. If it doesn't work, we move on to a different plan. And we'll keep doing that until we get the outcome we want."

I know he's trying to reassure me, but I don't think anything will. I won't be able to inhale a full breath until Hallie's in my arms again.

"Do you trust Bill?"

Jack appears in the doorway, blocking the space entirely. His blond hair is messily fastened, and his beard is wild and ragged, as though he's given up on taking care of himself until this situation is resolved. He heard my question and West's response.

"I don't trust Bill, but he knows me. He knows that I won't rest until this is over, and he can either end up on my side or …" He trails off and doesn't make any attempt to finish his sentence. Jack's huge hand grips the rifle and raises it slightly. I draw my own conclusion and a shiver that's more anticipation than fear passes up my spine.

He's on my side and prepared to do whatever it takes.

Hope becomes less of a firefly on the horizon.

"And Shona?" I ask.

"She's here for a chance at revenge," West says simply. "We won't let her get into a position where she can hurt you or Hallie."

"What about you?"

He frowns. "Focus on what's important."

I press my palms to my temples, overwhelmed at what's coming. "You are important, all of you."

His nod is slow, and his eyes soften. "We know what we're doing, Skye."

I focus on each of them: Jack's jaw that's set like concrete, Finn's straight posture and soft eyes, and the concerned furrow between West's brows. I memorize them like this. Strong and beautiful. Toughened by life but loyal and protective when it counts.

I wish I could do more. Be more. Deal with this on my own as I planned, but I have to face the facts. In a year, Hallie could be long gone. If I wait, I might never get her back.

It's not something I'm prepared to risk. I'll do whatever it takes. I'll let them become my saviors. I'll stand by while they do something so momentous for me that I'll owe them for life.

"I'll pray," I say. "For you all."

I might be helpless, but that's one thing I can do.

They nod, accepting my small offering gratefully.

When they leave my room, I drop to my knees and whisper to God, the Universe, Fate, or Mother Earth—whoever has the power—to protect the three lumberjacks who bought me for their pleasure but now risk their lives to save me and the daughter I love.

CHAPTER 20

JACK

LOOSE ENDS

"There are three of them," Finn whispers into the receiver. "Traveling in a chrome-colored Cadillac Escalade." Just like Skye and Shona predicted. Carter doesn't trust many people. Devon Webster and Keith Morgan are the only ones he trusts enough to get close to the big money.

They're both known to Bill and are wanted alongside Carter Reynolds.

This setup is as much a benefit to Bill as it is to me. To us.

He agreed to the extra clause I added to the terms and conditions late last night as the only way we can reach equilibrium. Once this is over, we're done for good.

"You're done there," I say.

Finn hangs up, and the line goes dead.

Now we know what we're dealing with, he can make his way back.

Three hours to go. The tracker Finn placed on the vehicle yesterday will confirm their exact positioning, so there won't be any surprises.

Except for Carter.

"Give me a whiskey, neat."

Reggie hands me the warm, amber liquid in a short glass, and I knock it back in one. His dark ringed eyes meet mine as he takes the glass, and I nod that it's time. He steps into the room behind the bar, and I watch as he flicks the switch, disabling the CCTV to the parking lot. The screens go blank. He pulls out the power cord to the box recorder and hands it to me. There's no way it can be powered on now. I didn't ask him to go this far, but I'm grateful I don't have to second-guess his loyalty. Stuffing it into my pocket, I lick the last taste of whiskey from my bottom lip. I could drink another shot, but I need my faculties sharp.

"Get that fucking asshole," Reggie says.

He's loyal to the men around here who put food on his table with their custom and provide backup when he needs it. That's the Shadow Outlaws, and us lumberjacks. But Carter propositioning his daughters who work behind the bar, scoping for fresh flesh for his shit hole of an establishment, has made this about revenge for him, too.

"We will."

I push my hair back from my face and secure it behind my head in a messy knot. A woman laughs as she drapes herself over Brian, who owns the local hardware store, and he runs his meaty hand over her exposed thigh. The music is loud, and a tune about freedom blares over the speakers.

So much is resting on me tonight.

My hands itch for an ax to swing but I head out into the darkness, instead, seeking the cool air to quiet my racing thoughts.

It's almost eight pm.

Everyone is in place, armed and ready with a mix of baseball bats, knuckle dusters, blades, and guns. The wind has died down, and the trees stand and wait like my comrades amongst them. Darkly dressed and well concealed, Aiden, Liam, Marcus, and Nathan are waiting for the signal. The lamps cast the area with just enough visibility for the lumberjacks to keep watch on the lot.

West is in the bar by the window, surveying the front of the building; we couldn't risk him outside after his visit to Carter's dive. He's there to keep a lid on Ethan who's going to play an important role tonight. Not that he knows about it. When the time is right, West will stage an argument with Ethan, and Reggie will throw him out the rear door. That will be the signal for everyone to move in.

The ambush will be totally unexpected.

Skye and Shona are upstairs in a back room, lying low.

I don't think Shona is a double-crosser, but Skye is armed, just in case.

Bones sits on his Indian Scout Bomber facing the rear door to the bar, a Viking of a man at the ready. He has removed his helmet and rested it on his knee as he waits. Lester and Arman flank him on either side, similarly armed and ready. They want this arsehole and his crew driven out of town on a permanent basis as much as I do.

There's a stash of cash tightly bound in a series of bundles in a case between Bones and Lester. It will be handed over when Carter delivers the anticipated methamphetamines in a quantity large enough to put the bastard and his crew away for a very long time.

Damn the motherfucker for bringing his filthy drugs into our forest town like he owns the place.

The irony of using Bill as part of the plan makes me smile. Amphetamines were his weakness back in the day, and his weakness cost me my career. My stepfather used them, too. He always fucked me up worse when he was coming off a high.

I think about Hallie and the danger she's in, living with a father like Carter. No child should be raised against this type of backdrop.

Carter's going to pay the price for all his actions tonight.

Rage courses through me at the misery he's caused Skye.

Clamping my eyes tightly shut, I grit my teeth, focusing on the bitter night air. I raise and drop my shoulders, relax my hands, and open my eyes to peer again into the darkness.

An owl hooting in the distance reminds me that this is my home, my turf. Skye and Hallie belong to me, West, and Finn now. It's time to set them free.

A dark Overfinch Land Rover Defender crawls slowly into the parking lot, its lights off but still decipherable under the low lighting.

It rolls smoothly over the gravel and takes up position in a back corner where the driver cuts the engine and sits silently, a shadow waiting in the darkness. The blackened windows conceal their occupant but offer him a clear view of the lot.

My right eye twitches involuntarily from exhaustion and anticipation. Adrenaline keeps me bolstered as I stand in wait at the side of the building.

Sweat trickles down my spine. I haven't felt like this since getting busted with Bill.

I force away a swelling rage, reminding myself that tonight is when I can begin to lay this ghost to rest. And maybe another.

The passenger door of the Defender opens an inch, and I stalk, concealed by the darkness, and hop up and inside in one stealthy move, closing the door silently. The interior smells like cigarettes and Bill's stifling brand of cologne. I rest my rifle down the side of my seat.

Turning to look at Bill, I narrow my eyes, wanting to find any kind of tell that he might be double-crossing me. It'd be a risky strategy, but Bill was never afraid of risk.

"After this is done, Jack, don't call me again. Are we clear?"

"Crystal."

The determination in his voice and his steady eye contact reveal everything I need to know.

We turn our heads to keep watch.

To wait.

He has aged since the photo I saw in the local rag cheering his promotion. Deep lines score around his mouth, and his neck has thickened. Neither of us is the same as we were before this job grounded the good out of us.

He betrayed me, but tonight, we'll call it quits.

He can return to his life in the force.

And I can return to mine in the forest.

I know who'll be happier.

The tracker's dot blinks on the map on my phone screen.

So close, it continues the last part of its journey. I shove the phone into my pocket and fix my eyes on the road.

Carter's chrome-colored Cadillac Escalade turns into the lot bang on eight-fifteen as had been agreed between him and Bones.

He's expecting to meet the Shadow Outlaws to seal the deal. They're getting the drugs for a reduced price if they tell him where Skye is. His desperate drive to find her and destroy her clouded his mind and made him sloppy.

The engine cuts, three doors swing open simultaneously, and all three men are immediately recognizable from the pictures.

Carter fucking Reynolds. Devon Webster. Keith Morgan.

This has to work.

Their heads swivel on the lookout for threats of danger.

I readjust my position in the seat.

Bill coughs but doesn't take his eyes off the prize. "Son of a fucking bitch."

I don't respond but take note of Carter's confident swagger. He's shorter than I expected. Another smile twists my lips.

I allow myself a moment to imagine my hands gripping tightly around his neck, choking, and squeezing the life out of him. In my imagination, his face glitches, becoming my stepfather and then returning to Carter's. Their sickening smirks match almost identically—two evil peas from the same degenerate pod.

The three men approach Bones and his sidekicks slowly. Devon and Keith finger inside their jackets where they're concealing weapons. They have parked close enough to minimize their exposure to anyone lurking in the parameter.

I glance at my phone. No call from West. They didn't bring backup. No need to resort to plan b. I power off my phone.

Carter's arrogant walk says it all. He thinks the Shadow Outlaws are small-time operators. He doesn't see them as a threat.

That's going to be a mistake that will cost him.

A brief conversation takes place, with Carter taking the lead. All six men in the scene throw their heads back and laugh at something he says.

Bill's ragged breathing is distracting. His lungs are fucked from smoking too much and doing no exercise.

Bones signals for Lester to lift up the case of cash. Carter looks back and nods to one of his men.

And then it all happens so quickly.

Ethan bursts out from the rear door of the bar, stumbling backward and losing his balance, crashing down with force against the ground and grunting at the impact.

The moment Carter and his goons turn to see the commotion, Bones pulls out a baseball bat and smacks it hard against the back of Carter's skull.

Lester and Arman draw weapons just before Devon and Keith can raise theirs. Carter falls to the ground, and I seize my moment and leap from the Defender.

The lumberjacks emerge from the tree line, roaring like savages, their numbers enough to make Carter's men falter. They lower their weapons and drop them to the ground, slowly raising their arms.

"Take the shit," Devon says as Lester grabs his arms and yanks them behind him.

"Take it and keep the money. We'll go. We don't want any trouble," Keith grunts.

So much for loyalty. I guess when you're an asshole like Carter, loyalty is hard to come by.

Carter groans on the ground, twisting in the dirt and clutching at the back of his head. Bones must have hit him hard. Not hard enough to kill him, I hope.

I get the sack over his head and shoulders as Arman, backed up by Nathan and Liam, hauls Devon and Keith until their faces press against the brickwork of Reggie's bar. West appears from inside, his rifle pointing menacingly at Carter.

Carter wriggles and kicks, crawling and moaning, but he's too concussed to resist. I drag his body over to Bill's car, and once I'm up against the Defender, I tie the sack firmly in place around his neck and reach into the car for ties to secure his hands and feet.

He's a small man but still a heavy half-dead weight. Bill doesn't help me get him into the trunk, but that's nothing new. Bill always was a selfish asshole.

I glance back at Reggie's. West is outside now. It's my

instinct to barrel into the fray and back him up, but that's not my role tonight.

When I slide into the passenger seat, Bill shakes his head.

"This fucker really pissed you off."

"He messed with someone important to me."

Bill nods and puts the vehicle into drive. We speed off, leaving nothing but a cloud of dust to prove that we were ever there.

Bill and I don't speak on the journey. Carter is livid at his capture, thrashing around as much as he can, making threats that he's in no position to carry out.

He thinks he's going to make me cower, but his ease with extreme violence only bolsters my conviction.

"You won't fucking get away with this, you fucking wasters. What the fuck is this?"

I snort, rubbing my hands over the worn denim encasing my thighs. My hands itch to squeeze Carter's neck until his eyes bulge and to hear him beg for his life.

"What do you want? Is it money? I've got plenty of fucking money. Name your fucking price." Although his voice is muffled through the sack and the car interior, the hint of fear and desperation rises in his voice with every word.

No amount of money would tempt me to release this man back into the world.

I flick on the radio, blocking his muffled shouts with upbeat country music.

Bill says nothing as he drives with one hand on the wheel, as though we're taking a trip to the beach. I watch the trees blink by, like a scene in a flick book.

My pulse intensifies with anticipation as Bill pulls up slowly at a bend in the road and turns in. The car jerks and dips over the gravely surface and eventually comes to a stop.

We turn to look at each other.

"I'll make the call." He pulls out the burner phone I

gave him.

I nod and leap out of the car, resting my rifle on the ground before I slam the passenger door and round the vehicle. Ripping open the trunk, I drag Carter out by his feet this time. His body hits the ground awkwardly, and he grunts with discomfort. "I've got a daughter. I'm a father. She's only a baby." He tries to keep his voice even, but there's a waver in it. Just the mention of Hallie has my blood boiling.

Bill turns the Defender and crawls away back down the trail. I watch him go as the beams get dimmer and dimmer until the vehicle speeds away.

At my feet, Carter starts to thrash and growl. I lift my right knee up at a right angle before jamming my foot into his gut with every ounce of strength I have.

He groans and curls in on himself as I issue a second kick to his shoulder, and then I drag his limp body further into the trees, pulling him into a kneeling position. All my anger, my bitterness, my resentment at the loss of my childhood at the hands of a man just like this one surges to the surface. Skye's broken and pleading eyes drift into my consciousness. The way her body shook as she sobbed at the loss of her baby.

It won't be difficult to do what needs to be done.

For her and for my own peace, I'd go to the ends of the fucking earth.

I return for my rifle before tearing the sack from Carter's head.

His eyes are wide, staring up at me as bloody drool drips from his split mouth.

The smell of his piss catches in the air.

Coward.

The night is dark, but the light of the moon casts a low beam, allowing us both a degree of visibility.

I'm glad he gets to see my face.

The shovel I left here earlier glints and the deep hole I dug yawns closely.

I wait.

"You don't have to do this." It's a whisper, a moment of gentle pleading from a man with so much blood on his hands and misery in his wake, he's heading straight to hell.

I lift his chin with the tip of my rifle.

At nine pm, the rumble of tires on the road and the glow of headlights creep toward me.

Bill is still listening to the country channel I selected, which amuses me. He was always more of a rock man. I open the rear door, checking that he's fulfilled the last part of the arrangement.

The car seat nestled in the backseat contains a sleeping baby with rosy cheeks covered by a soft pink blanket.

My heart squeezes in an unfamiliar way that tightens my throat.

Amongst all the darkness in the world, there is innocence and beauty.

I haven't had much of it, but that's about to change.

I close the door as quietly as possible, wanting to avoid waking our precious cargo, and climb into the passenger seat. Bill passes me the burner phone that I'll destroy later.

His eyes drop to my rifle as I place it next to me.

He was my partner. A man I should have been able to trust with my life.

He doesn't ask, and I don't tell.

We all have secrets that we'll take to the grave.

So, instead of making conversation, we head into the trees and towards the cabin.

Toward a new life.

The lights are on, and the curtains are open. The lodge illuminates the tree line around it like fire embers in a dark hearth.

West's truck is here. Shona's Corolla is gone.

Bill stops the Defender fifty feet away and keeps his eyes fixed in front.

"We're square?"

"Yep."

He nods.

As I step out onto the fallen leaves, and the wind whips around me, I prop my rifle against the car. I open the rear door and fumble to free the car seat from the belt. There are many things that I'm an expert in, but babies and their gear aren't one.

Hallie stirs but doesn't wake, even as I lift her weight and begin the short trek home, clutching my rifle in my other hand.

I don't look back as Bill's car crunches away until all I hear is the distant rumble of its engine.

My rifle is placed out of sight, having no place in a moment that should be filled with joy.

Hallie sighs sweetly, and I glance up at the sky, wondering how I ever deserved what's waiting for me inside. The stars twinkle hopefully, blinking as clouds temporarily obscure them, a flicker of hope in a sea of darkness.

This is going to be a new beginning for us all.

I carefully open the door, noticing that it is not bolted and feeling a jolt of relief. There's nothing to fear anymore.

As I enter the cabin, Skye, West, and Finn all rise to greet me, and Skye's eyes widen as she takes in the baby sleeping sweetly despite the circumstances. Her hands fly to her mouth as she stumbles forward, her knees going out from under her as she approaches Hallie. I rest the car seat on the floor, and Skye's hands hover over her baby as though she's afraid to touch her. She twists to look up at me, awe, and gratitude in the raise of her brows and her watery eyes. "She's mine again?"

"She was always yours."

And then it's like Skye has finally realized that she's free of Carter, free of his oppression, free of his evil. Her fingers fumble with the buckle and straps, finally getting them open, and she scoops Hallie into her arms, pressing her into her chest and nuzzling her sweet head. She stands and moves like a momma, bouncing Hallie rhythmically, even though she's miraculously still sleeping. Skye's wide, happy eyes sweep the room, taking in Finn where he's leaning against a chair, a relieved smile on his face.

West is standing nearby, his legs wide, still braced for the fight we found ourselves in.

"Where's Shona?" I almost forgot that her car was gone.

"She headed back to her place right after the bust. But we're expecting her in the morning."

"Any other wounded?" I ask.

"Only Ethan. He's in the hospital getting fixed up, so he shouldn't be a problem."

I cast my gaze back to the reunion scene in front of me and try my best to relax.

I take one final glance out the window and into the night, even though I know there's nothing out there in the vast, dark woods that will hurt us.

The wolves are all gone.

And our girl and her baby are safe with us forever.

CHAPTER 21

SKYE

BIRDS FLYING HIGH

Hallie stirs in my arms, and I can't take my eyes off her as her eyelids flutter and her pretty green eyes blink open. She fixes on my face, and for a few seconds, I can't breathe. Will she know me? Has our time apart fractured our bond forever.

I'm as anxious as I was when she was first born, fussing over every little sound she made, pressing my face close so I can feel her breath on my cheek.

Her chubby little hand reaches for my face and tangles in my hair, pulling. She doesn't smile, but she's always grumpy after a nap until she has time to get used to her surroundings again. I rest my cheek against hers and hum 'Hush, little baby' the way I used to before. When she nuzzles into me, I feel like my heart will break all over again.

It doesn't feel real. To hold her weight in my arms. To feel her warm little body and listen to her little noises. We've been apart for a month, but it feels like forever.

Finn comes closer, resting his palm against my back and gazing down at Hallie. I stare up at him, so uncertain about everything.

Hallie's back, but what will it mean for us?

When these men bid on me, I didn't come with baggage. All I arrived with was a purse and the clothes I was wearing. Now, I come with a dependent. This has to mean that I've broken the terms of the contract, and that will mean no money.

Before the panic squeezing my guts can rise and swell, Finn presses a firm kiss against my forehead. "I'm so happy for you," he says. "I'm so happy we could work this out for you."

I twist Hallie so that he can see my pretty baby. "This is Finn," I tell her as he reaches out to let her grab onto his pinkie. Her fingers are so tiny compared to his.

West approaches, too, resting his hand on my back. He kisses the top of my head and brushes back a stray piece of Hallie's hair that is tickling her eyes. "She looks just like you."

"You think?"

I always hoped she'd take after me rather than Carter, but he loved to tell everyone how much she looked like his mother, as though my connection to her was weaker than his.

Stop thinking about Carter, I tell myself.

They've made sure he's never going to bother us again. They did exactly what they promised, and my prayers protected them all. It's time to look forward, not back.

I search for Jack, finding him leaning against the wall with his leg bent and foot pressed against the plaster. I'm surprised to see him smiling softly. "Jack." I make my way to him, so overwhelmingly grateful for all he's done: the planning, the worrying … everything.

"Meet Hallie."

His bemused eyes sweep over Hallie's chubby cheeks and her little button nose. He gently reaches out his work-roughened palm and rests it on the top of her head as though he recognizes how precious and fragile she is. He quickly steps back.

"Thank you," I whisper, then turn to Finn and West. "Thank you."

"We protect what's ours, Skye. That's all you need to know. And you and Hallie, you're ours now. You don't ever have to worry about anything."

I blink, so surprised I have to swallow the ball of tears that wedges itself in my throat.

"I take care of what's mine, too," I tell them. "This home … all of you. It's the only place I want to be."

Jack presses off the wall again and wraps his arms around me and Hallie, and it's the first time I've ever felt truly safe. West and Finn approach and I'm passed from man to man, held securely in burley, solid lumberjack arms.

I cry because happiness and relief well up like a geyser breaking free. They brush away my tears, kissing my damp cheeks, telling me that I'm everything they ever hoped for but never believed they'd have.

I'm empty and broken, but I emerge from their embrace, healed and full of love.

Hallie starts to fuss, and we all laugh as relief over spills.

"I should sort her out. Maybe her diaper needs changing."

"Probably. Bill can handle a lot, but diapers aren't on his resume."

West reaches for a bag resting on the dining table and hands it to me. "I think I got everything you need, for now, at least. We can head into town tomorrow if anything's missing."

When I first met him, he shopped for me. Now he's shopping for my baby girl. Who would have guessed that a badass ex-military lumberjack would have such outstanding retail expertise?

In the bedroom, I lay Hallie on my comforter and empty the bag behind her. There are wipes and diapers, baby shampoo and bath products, a small towel and sponge, a comb, and a small tube of ointment. There are also a couple of sleepsuits in her size and the size up and a small stuffed bear with a sweet smile on its face and a tree on its little shirt.

I pass it to her, grinning as she grasps the bear with two chubby hands. "All it needs is a little pretend ax," I laugh as she immediately stuffs the bear's ear into her mouth. I undress her from her outfit, checking over her little body, holding my breath until I'm sure she's free of bruises and harm. She's lost a little of her baby chub in the past month, but maybe that's because I couldn't feed her anymore. I rest my hands over my breasts, wishing my milk to return, but it's long gone.

Once I've cleaned her little bottom and secured her into a fresh diaper and sleep suit, I return to the kitchen. Jack, West, and Finn are all seated around the dining table, speaking in hushed rumbles that stop when they see me.

There is a lot about tonight that I know they have no intention of sharing with me, and I'm okay with that. Our lives begin today, and everything in the past can stay dead and buried as far as I'm concerned.

On the table, is a box of baby bottles and four tins of formula, ready for hungry Hallie.

"Who's going to hold little miss while I fix her some milk?" I ask.

West is quick to hold out his hands, and I let him take her by the waist and watch with warmth as he rests her on his knee and bounces her gently. Finn and Jack look on with soft eyes and sweet smiles as though my little girl has chased the darkness from all their souls and replaced it with gentle affection.

I'm quick to clean the bottles and fix the warm milk, and I reluctantly let West feed Hallie, knowing how important it is for them to feel part of this. It's so sweet to see her stare at his handsome face, shadowed by his dark beard but lit up by his fascinated smile.

Finn wraps his arm around my waist, pulling me into his lap. Jack rises to fix us drinks. Whiskey for them and spiked hot chocolate for me. He even plates up some chocolate biscuits, which we devour as they ask me questions about Hallie's first few months and when she'll be walking and talking.

"What do you think about having more kids?" Jack asks me.

Finn opens his mouth to chastise him, but I reach out for Jack's hand across the table. "I want a big family," I say. "A really big happy family."

His eyes light up in a way I haven't witnessed before, and he squeezes my fingers before letting them go and resting back against the back of his chair.

"That's good," he says softly. "That's really good."

Later, when Hallie is sleeping in my bed, surrounded by pillows, I shower and pull on one of Finn's old shirts, buttoning it just enough to keep me decent. I pad into the den, finding Jack in low-slung plaid pajama pants and West and Finn in boxer briefs, spread out on the couch and chairs surrounding the fire.

Music plays in the background, something with a soulful country twist. The lighting is muted, coming only from a lamp in the corner and the flicker of flames in the hearth.

They laugh at something I don't catch, but it quickly dies when they see me.

"Hallie's settled," I say, resting my butt on the arm of the sofa.

"That's good." West's heated gaze slides from my toes to the top of my thighs. When he licks his lips, my sex clenches.

Finn wraps his arm around me and tugs me into his lap, quickly realizing that I'm not wearing anything underneath the shirt he generously gave me.

"Holy shit," he says as the fabric falls open, revealing my bare breasts. His hand slides up my leg to cup my naked ass as his mouth finds mine.

It's a sweet kiss that turns heated like the strike of a match.

When I slide my hands into his soft, blond hair, he makes a plaintive sound in his throat. Then, driven by a need he can't restrain, he stands with me draped across his arms and strides through the house. Two sets of heavy footsteps follow us down the hall, and somehow, Finn manages to kiss me until I'm on my back, splayed in the middle of his bed.

He kneels between my legs as West and Jack flank him on either side.

The first night I arrived at the lodge flashes into my mind. I was so scared. Scared that they'd hurt me. Scared I wouldn't be enough to please them. Terrified they wouldn't keep me or that I wouldn't make it until the year was up and I could get my money. I buried so many other fears, too. That Carter would find me, that he'd hurt Hallie, that I'd never see her again.

None of those fears are with me now.

The need to bury my hurt with pain and pleasure is gone, and all that's left is heated desire and something softer. A craving to be held by the three gruff lumberjacks who bought me and risked everything to keep me safe.

As Finn unbuttons my shirt, baring my body to three sets of hungry eyes, I marvel at how fate has directed me to this place and to these men who've become my rugged heroes.

Finn presses his mouth between my legs, so hungry to taste me that he emits a pained groan. His thumbs dig into my thighs, keeping them wide, holding me down, but my hips writhe against the flick of his tongue and the suction of his lips. I melt against the warm comforter as he takes me apart, piece by piece, then puts me back together. I clench around nothing, grasping the sheets, desperate for the weight of his body, the press of his cock to fill me, the frantic urge that will drive him to his release. Jack grips my chin, forcing my eyes open to focus on him. He kisses me with a fierceness that tears at my heart, his hair tickling my forehead and cheeks, soft against the hardness of the rest of him. West's hands caress my body, fingering my nipples, squeezing my breasts.

They play me like an instrument of pleasure, and I open to them, my body, my mind, my heart.

They gave me back my life, and now I'm ready to give them everything I am.

"Please," I murmur against Jack's lips, and he licks a stripe up my jaw then whispers darkly, "We can take you all at the same time."

"Yes," I gasp, already imagining the press of their powerful bodies against my softer flesh, the warmth of their skin, the flex of their muscles, the sweat and the heat, the yearning, and the burning.

Jack pulls a bottle of lube from Finn's top drawer and sits on the edge of the bed. He coats his cock in it, the slickness making his rough pulls sound even more explicit.

"On your back," he orders Finn.

We shuffle around until I'm straddling his lap, and he lowers me onto his waiting cock. I'm wet as a river, but the stretch still burns. The elasticity of my arousal begins to expand again. West's hand presses against my back, urging me to lean forward closer to Finn's chest. His thumb grazes my bottom lip as he fists his cock. I know what he tastes like, and I crave it like a drug that's weaseled its way into my psyche so deeply, I'll never be free.

The bed shifts behind me as Jack takes his place.

We can take you all at the same time.

My agreement was instantaneous and without thought, but I freeze as cool lube trickles between the cheeks of my ass.

His thumb presses against my taint, not a new sensation, but it feels different now there's a different intention behind it. I clamp down, and he laughs darkly. "Relax, Skye. You can take it. You can take us all."

West brushes the seam of my lips and touches my jaw, urging me to open and take him. All my concentration moves to what it feels like to have Finn and West inside me. Finn's hands stroke down my ribs and over the cheek of my ass as Jack's thumb breaches deeper, moving and stretching.

It shouldn't feel good, but invisible threads of sensation seem to connect parts of my body in terrible and beautiful ways only these men know how to find.

"Jesus," Finn gasps. "She gets so tight when you do that."

"She's about to get tighter."

The first press of his cock against my taint is shocking. It feels like the end of a baseball bat. Jack's hand glides up my spine, soothing, soothing.

"Relax," he croons. "You can do this. You can be what brings us all together."

Oh god. Jack's words almost wrench out my heart.

West's hand cups my cheek, and he withdraws his cock from my mouth. "Ready?" he asks.

"Yes." I groan deeply as Jack breaches and enters me. It doesn't hurt as such. It feels as though I'm being turned inside out and upside down. Finn's eyes are tightly closed, and his fingers press deeply into my flesh as he fights to maintain control.

The weight of Jack's body over me becomes greater as he leans into the penetration. I breathe in through my nose and out through my mouth, lowering my lids so that I can dwell in the darkness until his hips press into my ass. He lets out a guttural groan.

"Take her mouth," he orders West, and then he starts to move.

I lose myself in the push and pull, the frenzied hands, and the controlled thrusts. Everything feels liquid, like I'm slipping under water, eyes open, mouth breathing, a mermaid buffeted by wave after wave.

Heat flares between my legs as my clit is ground against Finn's pubic bone, and I'm filled beyond my comprehension.

West's hand in my hair grips tight enough that I see stars. Jack's hips jerk. Finn groans.

They're losing control because of me.

The rush of power is heady.

"Fuck." Jack crowds me, wrapping his arm around my chest and fingering my nipples until they ache. I'm so close to coming that I gasp as my hips move in tight jerks to push me over the edge. The clench of my pussy and mouth raises a collective shout. Cocks pulse, and I swallow West down as Jack and Finn tense with their release.

West drops back against the bed, cupping his dick, his expression wild and possessive.

I drop against Finn as he cradles me against his sweat-slicked skin. His beard tickles my forehead, and his hands make mesmerizing circles on my back.

Jack pats my ass as he slowly withdraws, leaving me suddenly empty. In a surprising moment of tenderness, he presses a soft kiss between my shoulder blades, his long hair tickling my skin and beard rasping.

West strokes my hair from my face, touching my puffy lips.

I'm wrecked and leaking their release, aching everywhere but feeling so viscerally alive that I get the urge to run into the freezing forest naked and shout to the heavens.

As Jack disappears to the bathroom and returns with a warm, wet washcloth to clean me up, I marvel at how free I feel within the bounds of a contract that has tethered me to three fierce lumberjacks who've turned out to be the best men I've ever met.

"You're safe now, Skye," Finn says.

West takes my hand in his, pressing featherlight kisses to my knuckles. "You'll always be safe with us."

Jack lifts my hair gently and nuzzles my neck. "Are you ready for us to keep you?" he asks. "Not just for a year, but forever?"

"Yes," I gasp.

His satisfied growl says it all.

And, as I lie between them, I realize that this is what it feels like to be home.

CHAPTER 22

FINN

SWEET BABY BIRD

Laying eyes on Hallie for the first-time last night and witnessing Skye scooping up her tiny daughter is a moment that will be etched in my memory forever. Skye's desperation and tension melted away in front of our eyes, and her tears were of love and joy rather than fear and anxiety.

Everything's different.

Last night, she truly let go with us, and it was beautiful.

I guess the difference is trust, first and foremost.

And love.

When she came here, she had no one.

Now she has her baby back and the three of us to keep her safe.

We're all connected.

It's morning now, and we're all watching Hallie sitting on her mom's lap, tugging West's beard with her chubby little hands. It's heartwarming to witness the change in Skye and hear the sweet laughter. Our cabin is alive because of it.

The release of stress and tension is like a balloon bursting.

"Time for breakfast," Jack says. He approaches the table with a plate overflowing with bacon, eggs, sausage, and toast. A feast for hungry men. In his other hand is a small pink plastic bowl that contains what can only be described as glop.

Skye lifts Hallie, places her on her hip, and carries her over to the table. We don't have a highchair for her yet— we need to travel out of town to purchase one—so Skye sits at the table with Hallie on her knee.

I heap food onto my plate, ravenous after last night's activities, and so does West, but Jack is focused on something else. He sits next to Skye, gently tucking a cloth into the neck of Hallie's romper and feeds her the glop. She's such a pretty little thing as she opens her mouth like a little baby bird, smacking her lips together as she consumes every spoonful.

Jesus. In a million years, I couldn't have predicted the strength of the man's paternal streak. He feeds Hallie breakfast with such tenderness and attention that I think he shocks himself.

So far, Hallie's not showing any signs of missing Carter. She's just so happy to be with her momma.

She's like a mini Skye, and they even have the same scent: something warm, sweet and addictive.

I plant a kiss on Hallie's chubby hand, and this time, it's my turn to have my beard tugged as she giggles and babbles away.

I want to keep this little girl safe, always, and forever.

As we finish eating, there is a knock at the door. West strides over to open it.

Shona enters more confidently than the first time she crossed the threshold and searches for Skye and Hallie.

When she sees them, her face lights up, and she strides across the room to kneel next to Skye.

Hallie immediately recognizes Shona and reaches for her, babbling about something we can't decipher.

Shona touches her hand gently. "There you are, baby girl. Back where you belong."

Skye beams and Hallie tugs the messy cloth from her neck, finished with her breakfast.

"Are you hungry?" West asks. "Jack went overboard on the food today."

"I'll take some coffee, black," she says.

As we sit around the table, talking and laughing at Hallie's baby talk and her love of beards, no one mentions Carter or what happened at Reggie's.

It's like it never happened, but it did.

Sometimes, we need to face up to our past, but sometimes, it's better to leave it buried.

We're drawing a line in the sand. The rest of our lives start today.

After an hour, Hallie begins to fuss and arch her back, ready for a nap already.

"I should go." Shona rises from the table and scoops up her bag.

"Where will you go?" Skye asks her.

"I'm thinking the West Coast. Somewhere hot. I'm done with the cold winters."

"I'll miss you," Skye says, bouncing Hallie to keep her calm. "Hallie will miss you."

Shona smiles sadly but makes her way to the door. "Be safe," she says.

"We will." Jack tugs open the front door, and Shona turns to smile at us all, raising her hand in a simple wave.

She pulls a woolen hat from her purse and tugs it onto her head. Then, with a simple nod, she leaves.

Skye disappears to put Hallie down for a nap, probably because she's upset. Shona's a friend, and it's hard to say goodbye.

I watch through the window as Shona climbs into her Toyota and drives away.

The last thread connecting Skye to her old life snaps.

It's December first, and Jack insisted on driving us all into town. Hallie's wrapped up snug in her stroller, and Skye is wearing an adorable pink fluffy hat that West bought her last week. The stores on Main Street are adorned with lights and festive decorations. Even Reggie has strung some lights around his bar.

West pushes Hallie's stroller proudly, and we're stopped along the way by Liam, who's laden with shopping, and Armen, who pulls up next to us on his motorbike, scaring Hallie with the rumble. Skye smiles sweetly when everyone comments on Hallie. She's such a proud, happy mom.

Jack disappears into a store, urging us to stay outside. After five minutes, he appears with a huge and very beautiful wreath. "For the cabin door," he says.

Skye reaches out to touch the sparkly red bow and touches Jack's arm in silent thanks. He pulls her into a side hug, kissing her forehead.

We're starting holiday traditions as a family and seeing my friends so deeply content is the best gift I could get.

As though the universe senses our holiday cheer, snow begins to fall gently from the white sky, dancing like glistening fairies. Hallie gazes up, blinking quickly as flakes get caught in her lashes. She sticks out her tongue and then giggles as the coolness registers.

Skye holds her hands out, catching disappearing crystals in her warm palms.

All around us, people stop and smile as the silence that comes with the start of snow settles on our community.

So much has changed since that day we drove to an auction, wanting to find a woman who could make our lives better. The things we thought we needed turned out to be secondary to what we've found to be the most important.

Connection. Affection. Love.

We might have bid on a woman, but what we truly found was a family.

And that is the most priceless gift of all.

EPILOGUE

JACK

A FOREST FAMILY

ONE YEAR LATER

"Daddy!" The sweetest sound snaps me out of my concentration zone, and I turn to see Hallie waddling along, wrapped in a scarlet red cape and a chunky white knit scarf made by her momma.

Her new sheepskin boots from Finn fit her perfectly, and her grin is wide. My heart flip-flops in my chest.

She tears off her hat and mittens, much to her momma's disapproval.

In her little jeans and with the sleeves of her checked plaid shirt sticking out from the red sleeves of her cape, she looks just like a mini lumberjack.

Skye's behind her, carrying a basket I know will be full of goodies for lunch.

"My angel!" I lower my ax to the ground and pull my

thick work gloves from my hands, dropping them to the forest floor. I stride towards my favorite girls, desperate for a taste of Skye's lips and a cuddle from Hallie. Stooping my head low to meet Skye's mouth with mine, I plant a lingering kiss, then turn to Hallie and scoop her into my arms.

She nuzzles into me, fitting perfectly into the curve of my neck, giggling as my beard rasps her sweet, soft skin.

She's as warm as a toasted marshmallow and smells sweet of freshly baked cookies.

"Daddy, so cold."

We laugh together, and her chubby little arms wrap tighter around me.

"Mommy and Hallie got lunch."

"Lunch!" I can't believe how many words she has now. "That's a big word, honey! I'm so proud of you!"

I'm excited to watch her develop and reach her milestones, but at the same time, I want time to slow down. It's a sensory and emotional overload. I love every sweet, tender moment.

"Mommy and Hallie make gingerbed."

"Gingerbread honey, gingerbread." Skye corrects her gently, but Hallie ignores her.

"Hallie want gingerbed."

With Hallie snuggled safely in my arms, we approach the trailer to share lunch with the rest of the crew.

Two other daddies will be as delighted as me to see their little girl.

Skye places the basket on the huge table that takes up most of the space in the trailer and lays out the contents.

The crew momentarily stop as they feast their eyes on the goods. The smell of freshly baked bread rises, mingling with a hint of pepper and spice from the winter-warming soup we all love.

Skye lays out parcel after parcel of carefully wrapped treats, and I catch her cradling her small belly with one hand.

The way to any man's heart is definitely through his stomach.

And his cock.

Although, giving him a baby trumps everything!

Hallie helps her momma lay out a series of tiny cupcakes topped with either light blue or baby pink frosting.

Hallie is buzzing with unspent energy and almost ready to burst.

The final item is a large carrot cake topped with extra cream cheese frosting, which has become one of our favorites and is usually a symbol of something being celebrated.

"You feeling all right, Skye?" Finn notices Skye being careful how she maneuvers around the table.

Her nausea has been hard on her the past couple of weeks.

"Course, Finn. It's just that feeding you ravenous men is no easy task. I read the other day that a lumberjack can need as many as seven thousand calories a day. It's mind-boggling!"

She's trying to detract attention away from herself and back to the boys waiting like pigs at a trough.

The basket makes a dull thud as she rests it on the floor and reaches her arms behind her to cradle the base of her spine.

"Mommy's baby is naughty…." Hallie giggles, and the room falls silent again.

The crew all look up from the feast as it slowly begins to sink in.

Smiles spread on their faces, and Aiden stands up and cheers when he sees Finn and West beaming at Hallie's comment.

Hallie starts clapping her hands together in delight, and before long, we are all toasting to the inadvertent announcement that Skye is expecting our baby. We found out last week but wanted to sit on the news until Skye had her first scan, which took place yesterday.

I take out the scan photo, which I've been carrying in the chest pocket of my shirt, close to my heart. I trace my finger around the tiny bean-shape who will be the next member of our family.

I'm so ready to cherish another tiny person.

One that will bond us all together by blood as well as love and loyalty.

For the first time in my life, it will mean something.

As the afternoon winds down, all I can think about is being back at the cabin with my family.

It seems like a lifetime ago that I was ruled by insomnia and darkness, driven by a desire for revenge and trusting nobody except West and Finn. All the wounds I carried made me sharp and bitter, but Skye has been like a healing balm, melting my heart and rebuilding my hope and belief that the world can be a good place.

The end of Skye's contract came and went.

We ordered her to keep the money, but she decided to buy things for the cabin to make it homier and a car for herself. She's put the rest into a savings account for rainy days, although I don't see her ever having a reason to spend it. We will always provide for her, Hallie, and the children we have.

Skye and Hallie have turned on the lights in our lives and given us all a reason to be.

West and Finn, as huge, lumbering, and macho as they are, have been reduced to soppy idiots most of the time.

Hallie loves to kiss the tattoos on West's arms and back and thinks they're like cartoons. She ruffles and pulls Finn's curls until his hair is like cotton candy. Hallie loves to grab my beard with both hands and pull my face down so that I can kiss the end of her sweet nose.

Finn was right to crave a woman's touch in our lives.

Skye brings us all to our knees but also makes us feel ten feet tall.

In five months, our family will grow again, and we're all ready for the changes that are coming.

My mom passed away a few months ago, and whilst I didn't ever get the chance to confront her about why she allowed my stepfather to abuse me, I decided that I would go to her funeral and offer her my forgiveness before slipping away unnoticed to return to my real family.

It was selfish really. A way to shed the last of the bitterness I carried in my heart.

I wanted it free to love.

I wonder if Skye's pregnancy will be the catalyst for her to reach out to her parents.

I try to imagine losing contact with Hallie and wince at the thought.

I won't pressure Skye. She'll know when the time is right. And she'll have our full support no matter what.

My carpentry has become something more than a hobby and a passion.

I've had items of furniture commissioned.

Ron Maggs is expecting his first grandchild and asked me to craft original bedroom furniture for the nursery. His daughter lives in one of the oldest and most beautiful houses in town and wanted me to provide something to reflect their home.

Word spreads like wildfire in this town, and more requests for bespoke wooden furniture have arrived steadily ever since.

We will have guests for Christmas this year. Shona is making a visit, and Aiden and his family are joining us for a festive meal. West has contacted a friend from his military days who's flying in especially.

I walk alone through the forest back to the cabin, but

I'm not lonely. Not anymore.

The frosty air I exhale forms plumes of smoke, but I'm warm on the inside. My body no longer aches from a lack of restful sleep but simply from tough physical labor. It's a healthy ache that I know will pass.

Now, I often spend my nights fast asleep with Hallie next to me, curled up like a little kitten. Her breathing is like a white noise that soothes any thoughts that creep back to torment me.

This Christmas, I will give her a small bed that I've been crafting by hand. It is almost finished.

I've carved her name into the headboard. Finn has decorated it with paintings of woodland scenes in vibrant colors. West has managed to find a shop in town that imports beautiful bed linen and has bought Hallie a set with a woodland fairy pattern. Skye has knitted her daughter a baby pink blanket with all our names woven in and plenty of space to weave in more.

The cot I made for Hallie when she arrived won't be empty for long.

The warm glow from the cabin up ahead makes me quicken my pace.

The throb of the festive music becomes more audible the closer I get.

My pulse quickens with excitement. I can't wait to walk through the door and begin to countdown to the holidays with my family. I promised Hallie that I would read her favorite story, "The Three Bears," at bedtime tonight. Emotion catches in my throat.

Skye's handmade wreath hangs on the front door.

It's a tradition I started last year and one that we will continue as our first family holiday tradition. I know we'll make many more as the years pass.

The warm air, scented with cinnamon and citrus, hits me as I walk through the door. The glow of the fire is a perfect backdrop to everyone as they all turn—laughing at something Hallie says—to welcome me back to them,

where I belong.
Where we all belong.

ABOUT THE AUTHOR

International bestselling author Stephanie Brother writes high heat love stories with a hint of the forbidden. Since 2015, she's been bringing to life handsome, flawed heroes who know how to treat their women. If you enjoy stories involving multiple lovers, including twins, triplets, stepbrothers, and their friends, you're in the right place. When it comes to books and men, Stephanie truly believes it's the more, the merrier.

She spends most of her day typing, drinking coffee, and interacting with readers.

Her books have been translated into German, French, and Spanish, and she has hit the Amazon bestseller list in seven countries.

Printed in Great Britain
by Amazon

40553467R00118